T0077311

Simon, Friends, and the Kidnapper

Book Two

by

R. E. Brémaud

Order this book online at www.trafford.com
or email orders@trafford.com

Most Trafford titles are also available at major online book retailers.

Printed in the United States of America.

ISBN: 978-1-4269-4554-0 (sc)
ISBN: 978-1-4269-4555-7 (hc)
ISBN: 978-1-4269-4556-4 (e)

Library of Congress Control Number: 2010915626

Trafford rev. 11/20/2010

North America & international
toll-free: 1 888 232 4444 (USA & Canada)
phone: 250 383 6864 • fax: 812 355 4082

Contents

Acknowledgments

I'd like to thank anyone and everyone who believes in this project and simply enjoys imaginative fiction and understands the value of dreams coming true.

I have a great amount of gratitude for the entire talented publishing team at Trafford for their time and energy spent on making my books a reality for me, my being published is my dream come true.

I dedicate this book to all who believe in making their dreams a reality, to my friends out there and my deceased mother who passed away in my opinion too soon.

Prologue

DreamRoyal castle
8:02 P.M

King Régimand DreamRoyal the tenth gets down on one knee after a dreamily fantastic meal prepared by Miss LossDream and proposes to her again. Miss LossDream squeals with dreamy joy, "Yes, oh yes I will marry you Régimand!" The King rises from his kneeling position and hugs his bride and future queen to be.

At the window is a peculiar character, like a shadow watching, listening, eavesdropping on their soon to be broadcast moment. He giggles with glee and waves to the others to come and see for themselves. One says, "Quick back to our spots they're leaving out the front door." They scramble and take their places in the DreamRoyal yard as they always do to avoid being caught.

At that moment, Simon Dreamlee walks up to his window and peers through his telescope at the Gargoyle statues and is perplexed by his findings. Simon's infatuation with these statues has expanded enormously eating up all of his spare time when he's not at Dreamtrue School, with Almont and Jilla or his parents or sleeping and dreaming. Simon's catalogued quite an observation book that he still will keep a secret from everyone in Dreamville. As he observes, one of the statues moves and Simon gasps at the sight. Those Gargoyles though have great hearing and the lion figure flies up to Simon's window and sprinkles him with the golden dust and makes Simon fall right to sleep and when he wakes up he'll have no memory of ever seeing the lion figured Gargoyle moving, flying or sprinkling dust on him.

The lion figure flies back to his spot and the lioness figure says, "She'll be angry you know, if and when she finds out." At that moment they all freeze as the DreamRoyal and Miss LossDream take a walk in the DreamRoyal orchard.

Chapter One – Looking Window Dream

Exactly one year and eleven days now since the terrifying week Miss DreamNot terrorized Dreamvillians by stealing their dreams, no one has heard or seen Miss DreamNot or the ex Dream Squad chief since their simultaneous banishment from Dreamville. The students of Dreamville sit in their seats in their respective dream inclined classrooms with their fellow colleagues in dream inclinations and download their dreams. The science inclined dreamers invent their technological gadgets and advancements based on the blueprints they dream to come true and the musically inclined dream of the notes and the theatre pieces with or without words. The artistically inclined dream about their latest paintings, sculptures, portraits, images, and designs to come true. The fashion inclined dreamers dream up new clothing styles to blow people's minds when they come dreamily true too. All in all, life in Dreamville has been nothing less than dreamy just as the founding ancients wanted the secret town to be. Dreamtrue School is the best school any student could attend with the best teachers and principal. After all, how many schools have an honorary, legitimate, direct descendant of a Royal family as their principal? King DreamRoyal the tenth kept his word and kept his post as the principal even though no one addressed him as principal. They all call him King DreamRoyal the coolest king of them all when they see or make any comments about him. He walks the corridors smiling, happy, encouraging and rocking the high fiving. Dreamvillians love their beloved King. It's safe to say, King DreamRoyal has made a triumphant return into the hearts of the citizens of Dreamville. In fact, Dreamvillians are super excited for the up and coming week, the week King DreamRoyal and Miss LossDream get married after their yearlong engagement.

Miss LossDream enters the musically inclined classroom, turns and faces the class, "Happy Thursday my dreamy students." The class replies simultaneously, "Happy Thursday Miss LossDream." Miss LossDream smiles and excitedly says, "My, my, the year has gone by. Not this Saturday but next Saturday, I'm going to be a bride, married, swept off my feet and carried over my permanent home's alter. I've sent you all my virtual invitations. Oh… I'll give you all a minute to read and then we'll start the class." Miss LossDream joyously walks to her desk and sits as the class reads their virtual invitation. Simon and Almont who now sit side by side look at their virtual note pads and the Royal invitation streams upward with golden letters on a virtual white scroll. Miss LossDream is a musically inclined dreamer and her wedding invitation begins to sing the words with the perfectly matched harp music emphasizing the words. The lady sings softly and elegantly but with just the right hint of joy to convey the dreamy message in the dreamy invitation.

A FAIRY DREAM ROYAL WEDDING COME TRUE
Fellow Dreamvillians, King DreamRoyal and Miss LossDream would like to
Cordially invite all of you to share in their dreamy golden Royal wedding
On the fourth Summer Festival Saturday at three in the afternoon when the sun is bright warm and dreamy
A perfectly dreamy day for a Royal dream wedding becoming true
We dream that all of you celebrate with us on this dreamy day, our dreamy dream Wedding day

King Régimand DreamRoyal the tenth
And
Miss Cédrina LossDream
(Soon to be the future
Queen Cédrina LossDream DreamRoyal)

The students all cheer and the girls all at once say, "Oh how romantic!" Almont says to Simon, "They'll kiss you know. They have to kiss at weddings." Simon says, "Just cover your eyes like I do and you'll be fine." Miss LossDream gets up from behind her desk and says, "Okay class it's time to share your dreams to come true. We'll begin with Simon Dreamlee. Simon, do you have any dreams you'd like to make come true?" Simon replies, "I have a very short, sort of funky, mainstream dream to share. It's actually not my usual type of music but here listen for yourself." Simon places his computer chip sized hand held computer in the pod and says, “Play my latest dream.” The large screen hovers down from the ceiling and his dream plays out on the screen. The music is funky with techno sounds of the outsiders primitive computers paired with the tin sound of keyboards and the classic beats of a real drum. The singer’s voice is a very cheery girl’s voice coolly belting out the words.

I woke up one morning
Happy, happy, oh happy day
Yeah, Oh yeah it’s a happy day in Dreamville
I’m singing
I’m dreaming in Dreamville
It’s a party in Dreamville
Party in Dreamville

Party, party, party
Party in Dreamville

I wake up every morning
Happy, happy, oh happy days
Yeah, Oh yeah it’s a happy day in Dreamville
I’m dancing
I’m making my dreams come true
It’s a party in Dreamville
Party in Dreamville

Party, party, party
Party in Dreamville
Party in Dreamville
Oh come and party with me

Party, party, party
Party in Dreamville
Party in Dreamville
Oh come and party with me

Simon’s funky hip hop song stops playing and everyone claps and cheers. Simon says, “Really… You guys really like it?” Miss LossDream says, “Yeah Simon. What’s not to like? It’s short, simple, upbeat and as you said very mainstream. It’s good. This dream will definitely come true and be marketed to the outsiders. Simon you're contributing really well to Dreamville's economy." Simon smiles and says, "Wow... that's great. I'm not going to lie though. I thought everyone would hate it. Seeing how it's so commercial." Everyone in his class claps and cheers, "Simon rocks! Simon rocks! Simon rocks!" Miss LossDream says, "Commercial, well everything's commercial now isn't it. How else do you expect to make money? Now class... Who wants to be the next to share their latest dream to come true?" Miss LossDream looks around the classroom at all the musically inclined dreamers while Simon says, "Pssst... Almont share your dream." Almont shakes his head to non-verbally indicate that he doesn't want to share his dream, unfortunately for him, Miss LossDream says, "Almont Alldream... Why don't you share your dream with us like your friend Simon Dreamlee suggested you do." Shocked, Almont looks at Miss LossDream and she says, "Acoustics... We hear everything in this room even the whispers of two boys who are not paying attention." Simon clears his throat and looks towards the front of the class at Miss LossDream who's smiling at him. She then turns her focus to Almont and smiles at him as well. She says, "We're patiently waiting Almont." Almont says, "Play my latest dream please." His dream starts to play on the big screen. The music has reggae beat with tin drums, flutes and a little guitar that match the soothing words of his new composition.

I'm traveling, traveling along the path of life.
Yes I'm traveling along the path of life.
I'm happy, happy to be alive.
Oh happy to be alive.

I'm traveling, traveling along the path of life.
Yes I'm traveling along the path of life.
I'm excited, excited to be with you.
Oh excited to be with you.

I'm traveling, traveling along the path of life.
Yes I'm traveling along the path of life.
I'm feeling, feeling loved by you.
Oh feeling loved by you.

I'm traveling, traveling along the path of life.
Yes I'm traveling along the path of life.

I'm traveling, traveling with you.
Yes I'm traveling with you.

Oh... I'm traveling, traveling along with you.
Oh just traveling, living for you.
Knowing I'm loved by you.
So I'm traveling, traveling along the path of life.
Oh... with you.

The music and the dream ends and the class cheers for Almont who begins to smile. Simon says, "That was great. Cool, smooth and soothing." Miss LossDream says, "Yes quite good Almont. I wonder, though, why were you so reluctant to share this remarkably good dream?" Almont looks at Jilla MusiDream and quickly looks back at Miss LossDream and replies, "I... I just kind of... Well..." Miss LossDream says, "Oh never mind Almont. I'll send this to marketing to get it sent to the outsiders. They'll call you to sign a contract when they've drafted one. Alright, who will be next? Oh there's the bell! "Ring, Ding, Ling, Ring!" Miss LossDream says, "Well I'll see you all tomorrow, Dreamator Friday. Sweet dreams!" She waves at the students as they all exit the classroom. Almont and Simon walk silently down the corridor and out the front door. Rino and Jilla are holding hands and walking in the direction of the DreamScifi's house. Simon says, "You're still head over heels for her huh?" Almont says, "Nah... Whatever... I've never liked her. I have no idea what you're talking about." Almont playfully and jokingly punches Simon on the shoulder. Simon says, "Owe... Okay, there's no need for violent behavior." Almont and Simon look at each and laugh at the little joke. "Ha! Ha! Ha!" King DreamRoyal and Miss LossDream observe them through the window of the front doors to Dreamtrue School. King DreamRoyal says, "Boys will be boys even still to this day." Miss LossDream smiles at him and they walk away hand in hand to do their after school work, rating, grading and submitting dreams to come true and to be marketed.

In the meantime, Simon and Almont run to their hover boards, climb on them and start hovering for their homes. Laughing, they race through the streets to their crossroads and go their separate ways. Almont yells, "See you tomorrow Simon!" Simon yells back, "For sure reggae man!" Simon hovers quickly towards his home. He no longer has a fascination with the black, decrepit house on the hill but he has a new obsession that compels him to still observe the DreamRoyal castle and surroundings. He quickly hovers up the hover way driveway and lowers his hover board into the solar panel grid in the backyard. He runs inside his house, runs past his mother and runs up both flights of stairs straight into the attic. He begins surveying the yard and particularly the golden gargoyles. He hasn't told anyone what he's observed or showed anyone what he's documented in his own hand writing either. Paying close attention to detail, he's noticed variations in the statues from time to time, which, intrigues him. His busy mind wants to believe that they are capable of moving around but without enough evidence he can't prove that they are in fact living, breathing, night creatures. Simon says, "Oh why did King DreamRoyal have to tell me that there's a legend regarding these interesting statues. Why I'm I so obsessed with the notion that I already know that they come to life?" Suddenly, he hears Mrs. Dreamlee say, "Simon, son, dear, come for supper." Simon replies, "Coming mom." He leaves his telescope pointing at the gargoyles and runs down the stairs to the kitchen. Simon's mom says, "Here Simon, strawberry short cake for supper with hot fudge chocolate sauce." Simon smiles and sits in his chair and they all begin to eat. Mr. Dreamlee listens and watches the virtual news. The media clown says, "It looks like another beautiful, sunny, cloudless, dreamy Dreamville day has went by as all Dreamvillians prepare to capture their next dreams come true. Sweet Dreams everyone!" His father turns off the virtual news and says, "Well son your latest dreams come true didn't make the news." Simon replies, "Yeah, I think it's because of the huge influx of marketable dreams that there's a slow reaction by the Dreamville media clowns." Mr. Dreamlee says, "Hmm… could be son. That very well could be." Mrs. Dreamlee claps her hands and the cleaning robots clear and cleans the kitchen until it's spotless. She says, "Well Simon go wash up and get ready for dreamtime." Simon gets up and runs upstairs to wash his face and hands. He walks to his bedroom and looks out into the backyard. Frankie Noodles rubs up against him for attention as cat tends to do so Simon pets his kitty, "Purr, Purr, Purr…" Boomboom Booya runs in his room and jumps on his bed making his spot a sleep haven fit for a dog, "Woof, woof…" Simon leaves his room and quickly runs upstairs to look out of his telescope into the night sky. Finished documenting all the constellations, he now searches for something else in the dreamily clear sky but there's as usual nothing. Simon says, "I'm not even sure what I'm looking for anymore." He hears footsteps coming upstairs to the attic and he quickly hides his documentations about the subtle nuances in the golden gargoyles appearances from time to time. Mrs. Dreamlee says, "Simon time for bed."

Simon gets up and sees his mother standing in the doorway. They walk downstairs to the second floor and Simon enters his room. She says, "Sweet dreams son." Mr. Dreamlee yells from downstairs, "Sweet dreams Simon, my boy." Simon replies, "Sweet dreams mom and dad." His mother shuts the door and Simon climbs into bed. He hesitates to put the dream catcher on his head but shaking the ridiculous, unfounded and un-necessary fear off, he attaches the dream catcher to his head and in Dreamville tradition, as soon as his head touches his pillow, he falls to sleep and dreams.

All Dreamvillians sleep soundly and snuggly in their beds. Including Simon, now thirteen but still short for his age, sleeps soundly in his bed with his dream catcher attached to his head and recording his latest dream, with the success of the sequel to King DreamRoyal and Miss LossDream's love story being produced and sold to the outside world and despite Simon being a classical musical inclined dreamer, his latest dreams that have come true since the controversial love story were very upbeat and trendy regardless of his usual inclination. However, tonight his dream once again is reverting back to classical music and a stage performance but it's oddly vivid and seemingly believably historical. Meanwhile, in the world of Dreamville where night creatures are awake, Gargantua the gargoyle flies by Simon's window and peers in his room. The half man, half lion sees Simon sleeping and says, "Little truth dreamer is asleep and dreaming peacefully." The gargoyle turns and waves a signal that all's well in Dreamville to the fifteen other gargoyles that accompany him through the night and while he's a motionless statue in King DreamRoyal's yard. Gargantua says, "Little truth dreamer I bid you sweet dreams." Gargantua flies away from Simon's window, he flies up the hill with all the others. They fly into their spots and strike poses as they wait for the sun to come up and harden their bodies and faces into golden glistening statues. Sleeping, Simon dreams of a time long ago when the DreamRoyals ruled Dreamville by overseeing every Dreamvillians dreams and supervising the Outsiders behaviors. His dream is vividly musical and classically inclined but also theatrically inclined as the play evolves throughout the night while he sleeps and dreams.

Simon's dream begins with flashes of large red numbers, first the number one, followed by the number three and then another three and finally the number eight indicating the year thirteen thirty-eight. The looking window in Dream Mountain is the next flash image in Simon's Dream and suddenly, people talking to each other instead of singing. A small man dressed in red and blue stripes materializes and says, "King

Régimand DreamRoyal the third, his queen Lélilla DreamRoyal and their loyal servants supervise, observe and help the outsiders on a regular basis from Dream Mountain's looking window." King Régimand DreamRoyal the third dressed in royal garbs of royal blue velvet, curly brown hair and reddish beard, says, "Among these different types of night creatures, I counted seven different types, two lions, two dogs, two wolves, two eagles, two snakes, two goats, and two monkeys. Seemingly, they're merely mixes of different types of animal body parts and human body parts. This combination creates these magnificent creatures. Do you agree Timatie?" Timatie is the small man dressed in red and blue stripes, he says, "I do agree sire. I also have observed that often the outsiders incorporate them into their primitive religions to warn their people to not underestimate the devil they fear so much." A woman dressed in deep purple velvet, whose raven black hair is adorned with a gold crown who could only be Queen Lélilla says, "Thank dreams we don't have anything terrible to fear here in Dreamville." King Régimand says, "No we don't have to fear anything here my dear but I fear for their lives. Unfortunately, the outsiders fear the statues of these wonderful creatures. Outsiders automatically fear what they do not understand and if they ever knew that they come alive and roam around the world at night, I think the outsiders would kill them. Worse, these creatures would not defend themselves. We have observed them be nothing but kind and gentle. They fly around at night almost as if they are guarding something. This makes it hard for me to believe that they're dangerous and evil like these outsiders say." Suddenly, the hidden rock door opens and another one of the king's loyal followers enters the room bows before his king and says, "King DreamRoyal, I found an ancient text describing these creatures. After carefully reading it, it turns out they are a dream that came true for one of the ancient families of magic inclined dreamers, Master MagicDream. He wrote the text just before he and his family voluntarily moved out of Dreamville to live in the Outside world making them automatically banished forever from ever re-entering into Dreamville. According to this ancient text, what we observe today is false. The outsiders have created their own false statues that resemble the real gargoyles but of course those ones do not come to life which is not a big deal but unfortunately the Outsiders have attached false, terrible and evil meanings to these false gargoyles creating the fear of them and the real gargoyles that we observe daily. Would you like to read it my king?" King Régimand DreamRoyal the third says, "You may stand Milany, pass it here and I'll transfer it to the big screen." King DreamRoyal inserts the book into a slot in the desk under the looking window and a screen descends down out of the rock surface for a ceiling.

The words of the ancient text materialize on the screen. King DreamRoyal says, "I shall read out loud the text written by Master MagicDream. He begins to explain that Lions are the most common non-native animal. I crafted two gargoyles, female and male, to look like a lion with the body of a human. In these times, the lion is linked to the sun, due to its golden mane bearing a striking similarity to the solar wreath of the sun. These two gargoyles shall be strength and endurance." Queen Lélilla DreamRoyal reads, "Here he explains, dogs are the most common native animal. Dogs are faithful, loyal, intelligent and excellent guardians. I crafted two, female and male, in the image of a dog with a human body."Timatie reads, "Although the wolf is feared by the Outsiders as well as the Dreamvillians, it's also a much respected animal. Wolves live and cooperate together as a pack making them capable of fighting off evil. I crafted two, female and male, in the image of the wolf with the body of a human." Milany reads, "The eagle's a powerful bird that's able to slay dragons. Their eye sight allows them to see incredibly far away objects. They possess the ability to renew themselves by looking into the sun which is why they always have a glint in their eyes. I crafted two gargoyles, female and male, in the eagle's image with the body of a human." King Régimand DreamRoyal the third reads, "The snake or the serpent is immortal because they shed their skin and rejuvenate themselves. I crafted two gargoyles, female and male, in the image of a snake with a human body." Queen Lélilla DreamRoyal reads, "The goat is strong and surefooted with the ability to climb mountains to find food. I crafted two, female and male, in the image of a goat with a human body." Timatie reads, "The monkey is intelligent, strong, and smart creatures. I crafted two, female and male, in the image of the monkey. I kept the monkey's body but made it larger and stronger." Milany reads, "I created these creatures as a gift to the Outsiders. They will live at night and protect them from any harm that may threaten them while they sleep. They'll no longer need to fear anything or anyone. I, Master MagicDream, hope that these gargoyles will alleviate and eventually destroy the Outsider's nightmares. Their haunting nightmares affect them during the daylight hours and, especially, while they're asleep at night. These needless fears hinder their existence. The one fear they have is proven to be nonsense and yet they fear it, him or her, the one they call the devil. My creations will keep this so called devil away." Suddenly they all hear a loud crash, mobs of people yelling and fires burning. The large screens floats upwards disappearing into the rock ceiling. They look out the looking window into the darkness of the night. The primitive outsiders, most unlike the ones today, are walking around with their pitch forks and torches of fire. They light the grass around the motionless and helpless gargoyles. King DreamRoyal says, "They're going to burn them to death." They watch in horror as they listen to the Outsiders sing about their hatred for the gentle gargoyles.

Simon sweats in his sleep as the music notes, treble clef, base clef, time signature, key signature, sheet music and lyrics appear and fill his dream along with images of the gargoyles being blackened by the burning grasses surrounding them as he too can see out of the looking window as if he were right there besides King Régimand DreamRoyal the third. Simon tosses, kicks, turns and rips his bed apart as he dreams through the second half of the night until morning with his new song resounding in his head in his dream.

Lions, symbols the deadly sin of pride
Lions no more we fear thee.
We will burn you and your witchcraft worshipers.
Burn, burn, burn and be gone.

Dogs can't resist the sin of temptation.
Dogs are always hungry, stealing food.
Dogs are sinners, thieves.
Burn, burn, burn and be gone.

Wolf, the devil's pet you are and we know.
Wolf, you are the deadly sin of greed.
Wolves are sinners and the pet of evil.
Burn, burn, burn and be gone.

Snake slithers, slides, and hides.
Snake is a sinner.
Snake symbolizes the deadly sin of envy.
Burn, burn, burn and be gone.

Goat, so cleverly disguised as cute.
Goats are the most evil sinner.
Goats represent the deadliest sin of lust.

Burn, burn, burn and be gone.

Monkey, stupid and ugly monkey,
They are nature gone awry to punish humans for their sins.
Monkeys are the living deadly sin of sloth.
Burn, burn, burn and be gone.

Burn, burn, burn and be gone.
Burn, burn, burn and be gone.
Burn, burn, burn and be gone.
Burn, burn, burn and be gone.

Chapter Two – Dreamator

The sunrise lighting Simon's room, he opens his eyes and detaches the dream catcher from his head. Simon says, "That was a strange dream if ever I had one." He gets out of bed, puts his dreamy hand held computer chip sized computer in his pocket and stretches his limbs. Simon opens his bedroom door and runs up to the attic. He looks out the telescope at the Gargoyles in King DreamRoyal's yard and takes note of any slight differences in the poses of the statues. Simons says, "Hmm… Interesting, the one with the lion's head and male body is facing the castle as usual but today, his eyes are looking at the castle and yesterday, his eyes were looking at an apple tree." Simon hears his mother calling, "Simon come down for breakfast." Having no time to observe any other discrepancies, he re-hides his observations in his tin box and runs down both flights of stairs. Boomboom Booya and Frankie Noodles come out of his room and run down the stairs along side of him. He runs into the kitchen and sits down for breakfast. He asks his mother, "So what are we eating this morning?" Mrs. Dreamlee replies, "Blueberry pancakes and maple syrup." Mr. Dreamlee says, "Yummy. Now, that's a great breakfast hey son." Simon smiles and his mother places the plate in front of him and his father and they eat until the plate is empty. Simon says, "That was great mom! Well I'm off to school, even though the focus is sports day today." Mr. Dreamlee says with a laugh, "Ha, ha… Don't worry son, us scientifically inclined dreamers aren't so athletic either. Just have fun!" He winks at his son. Simon smiles and says, "Yeah well I'll do just that even though I already know what the outcome of this event will be." Mrs. Dreamlee asks, "What sport are you playing?" Simon replies, "I have no idea. I think Miss LossDream mentioned it but I didn't pay attention. Frankly, I rather share my dream today because the one I just had is strange, weird." Mrs. Dreamlee says, "Well… happy Friday to you, son!" He replies, "Happy Friday mom and dad." Simon walks out the back door from the

Kitchen and steps on his hover board. He starts to hover towards the front yard towards his street and hovers for a brief moment at the end of the hover driveway to look up at the DreamRoyal castle. The structure of multiple golden bricks and rocks glisten in the sunlight. Simon smiles to himself and starts hovering towards the crossroads of Dreamway Street and ValleysDream Drive, where every school day morning, Almont meets him. Simon reaches the crossroads and waits in a still hover mode for Almont to arrive. He pulls out his virtual communicator and says, "Dreamville's news." The media clown appears and says, "Dreamvillians can expect a fabulously dreamy sunny day with not a cloud in sight. As for no clouds in sight, there certainly are none in sight for two of Dreamville's finest musically inclined dreamers, Simon Dreamlee and the little less famous Almont Alldream and their dreams come true. Their latest mainstream hip hop and reggae songs have been successfully marketed and dreamily reportedly, the Outsiders love the songs to bits. Congratulations boys and happy Friday." Simon says, "Shut off." His virtual communicator shuts off and he hears Almont's hover board in the distance. He sees Almont now who's waving frantically at him. Almont gets closer and yells, "Oh sorry dude, I slept in this morning. Thanks for waiting." Simon and Almont start hovering towards Dreamtrue School. Along the way every one of the adults wave, smile and congratulate Simon and Almont on their latest dreams. Mrs. Dreammore and Mrs. LandDream say, "Congratulations Simon. Congratulations Almont." Simon replies, "Thank you Mrs. Dreammore, thank you Mrs. LandDream." Almont says, "Yeah thanks!" Mr. BottomDream says, "Good job chaps." Simon replies, "Thanks Mr. BottomDream." Almont says, "Thanks Mr. BottomDream." They reach DreamHappy Street, hover into the hover parkade and lower their hover boards into the solar panel grids. Simon says, "Well here we are at Dreamtrue School ready to get slaughtered by all the sports inclined dreamers." Almont says, "Yeah I know. I mean why do we have to participate? It's obvious we're not athletes." Simon raises his hand in a high five motion and Almont reciprocates. They both say, "To getting slaughtered" as they high five each other. They run out of the parkade, down the cement sidewalk, down the corridor and into their classroom. They quickly sit in their seats at their desks just as Miss LossDream enters the relatively silent classroom.

Miss LossDream looks at the class and says, "Happy Friday!" The class replies in a beautiful tone and all at once, "Happy Friday Miss LossDream!" Miss LossDream says, "Well today there are no regular classes because it is the once again newly introduced sports day in Dreamville. It's been eleven years since we've had a sports day in Dreamville. As a class we will make our way to the Dreamville coliseum. Now if you all will simply follow me." They all line up behind Miss LossDream and follow her into the gymnasium. Simon says, "Coliseum but this is just the gymnasium." King DreamRoyal enters the gymnasium with the rest of the dream inclined classes and he tells everyone in a firm voice, "Stand back against the wall." Everyone, leans against the wall piling on top of each other as King DreamRoyal says, "Reveal for the Dreamator day." As he finishes his words the room begins to shake, the floor begins to move, the walls fill with seating for spectators and the floor retracts into the walls to reveal more surface seating and a playing field. All the students are amazed, "Wow, awesome. Cool… Rocking…" Simon says, "I love Dreamville." Finally the roof disintegrates and the indoor school gymnasium is turned into an outdoor sports coliseum. Almont says, "I wonder what sport we're going to be forced to play." Simon says, "Ah just have fun!" King Dream Royal says, "Now everyone find your seats in the stands and wait while the sports inclined coaches consult with each other." Everyone sits in their seats with their fellow similar inclined dreamers. The increasingly growing impatient crowd of students begins to fiddle with their virtual communicators and hand held computers making a lot of noise. Almont stares at Jilla and Rino who've somehow managed to end up sitting together kissing and smooching. Almont says, "Ugg… Don't they ever quit smooching?" Simon says, "Here's an idea send Jilla a really long virtual message to distract her from Rino." Almont says, "That's a great idea. But what do I send?" Through all the noise King DreamRoyal's amplified voice aided by talking into his virtual communicator says, "ATTENTION, YOUR ATTENTION PLEASE!" The students put away their gadgets and quiet down to listen to what he has to say to them. King DreamRoyal says, "Thank you my dreamy students. I now turn your attention over to the Dreamville coaches, Mr. and Mrs. DreamCoach." Mr. DreamCoach walks up to the students and says, "Welcome to Dreamville's dreamy sports Friday. We'll play the sport most unique to Dreamville, Dreamator." Suddenly, a bunch of balls of all sizes materialize on the floor and then, ten, meter long by meter width sized trampolines materialize between the balls. Each trampoline has a basket hanging above it. Almont says to Simon, "Actually, I like Dreamator." Simon nods his head and says, "I still don't know how to play." They look back down at the game field and they see hovering disks appear above the baskets. The coach says, "Okay the game field is ready. I'll go over the rules with you. Now, listen carefully. Rule number one, only the dream scorers can use their hover boards. Rule number two, only the dream scorers pick up the balls off of the floor and make a basket worth ten points each. Rule number three, only the dream scorers have the difficult task of distinguishing the real balls from the virtual balls. Rule number four, for each virtual ball they pick up their team loses five points. Rule number five, only the dream blockers have baby clubs. Rule number six, only the dream blockers can jump from trampoline to trampoline to block their opponent's attempts to score points in their team's baskets. Rule number seven, only the dream blocker of the opposite team can shatter the protective hovering disk that hovers above each basket to block the balls. Rule number eight, they must shatter these disks with the same club. Rule number nine, the dream blockers must not touch the floor or the game is forfeit and automatically won by the opposite team. Rule number ten, the dream scorers must not fall off of their hover boards. Rule number eleven, all teams have to be five players, two blockers and three scorers. Now, the object of the game is to shatter the opponent's five hovering blocking disks before the other team to win the game with a whopping one hundred and fifty additional points added to your team's score on top of the points scored by the dream scorers. At the end of the tournament, the winning team wins the Golden Dreamator trophy." The students cheer as the coach raises the trophy in the air. It's an oddly shaped trophy with the golden statuesque image of a boy and a girl on a hover board with balls in their hands. The coach says, "Now let's have a good clean tournament and remember the basket automatically calculates the points with each ball that gets put inside and automatically deducts points if a virtual ball gets put in it." King DreamRoyal says, "Okay my dreamy students, your dreamy teachers will name your classes' team. If... if you're not nominated then cheer, cheer for your team." Simon and Almont wait for Miss LossDream to stand up and nominate their musically inclined dreamer's Dreamator team. Jilla says, "Miss LossDream seems to be doing some kind of calculations." Startled, Almont says, "What are you doing up here when you were down there with your boyfriend, Rino, smooching Rino." Jilla replies, "He's preoccupied with his science inclined dreamers team. He was named team captain and head scorer." Almont says, 'Of course he was. I mean he's damn near perfect isn't he." Jilla sighs and says, "Sigh... he is perfect." Almont says, "Ugg... he's a little old for you being that he's turned fifteen and you're only twelve." Jilla says, "I turn thirteen this Monday." Simon hushes them both, "Shush, Miss LossDream is standing." Almont says, "She's about to announce the team members."

All the coliseum is silent as each teacher announces their classes team members to their students. Miss LossDream says, "Now class I've taken this into considerable consideration and I've thought and re-thought about who should represent the musically inclined dreamers this year and I've decided to nominate five of you that I think will benefit from the experience regardless of whatever the outcome may be in the end. Now, I want everyone to remember to have fun and cheer on your team. The members are, Brian Dreamery as head dream scorer and captain, Hughes Dreamy as second dream scorer, Nick Daydream as the third dream scorer. As for the dream blockers, I've nominated Jonas Dreamsound and lastly Simon Dreamlee." Almont pats Simon on the shoulder and says, "Good luck!" Jilla says, "You'll do fine." Simon makes his way to Miss LossDream and says, "Miss LossDream, are you sure you want me to play? I mean I'm not exactly athletic." Miss LossDream replies, "You may not think so but if I recall correctly, when I attended school with your mother, she was quite the talented dream blocker. You should take a look on the trophy. You'll read her name on the plaques of the trophy under her maiden name of course, FashiDream." Simon replies, "Of course." He turns around not realizing that Almont and Jilla had both followed him and heard what Miss LossDream said. Jilla says, "Wow, Simon not only are you musically inclined, scientifically smart but you're also potentially athletic too." Almont says, "Yeah dude, that's great." Simon hesitates to say, "Yeah that's really great." Simon realizes that he may not be as good as his mother and if he isn't he'll be letting his whole team down. His nerves are beginning to make him nervous, hot and sweaty.

Simon sees his team mates make their way down to the playing field and being directed into the dressing room area. He runs down saying, "Excuse me, sorry, pardon me, thank you." He goes into the dressing room area and sits with his team mates. They sit quietly as they are handed their team jerseys by Miss LossDream. She says, "They should all fit you." The jerseys are purple and red, two passionate colors for passionate musicians. Each jersey has their names embroidered in white on the back and the Musical Dream Team embroidered in white on the front. All the team's sit silently putting on their jerseys when Miss LossDream says, "Okay everybody here's your protective gear, knee pads, elbow pads, helmet, and miniature clubs for the dreamy blockers." They continue to strap on their gear without speaking when the broken silence fills with the voice of coach

DreamCoach. He says, "All enjoy the dreamy Dreamvillian traditional game of Dreamator. The mounting anticipation to find out who will win this dreamy tournament fills our dreamy Friday day. So go out there and play hard." The players start giggling as their attentions are drawn to thirteen year old Simon Dreamlee, the shortest, youngest musically inclined dreamer to be named to the newly formed Dreamator team when he softly says, "These pads are falling off of me." He then clears his throat, looks at Miss LossDream, she signals to everyone to stop laughing with a simple gesture of her hand and everyone stops giggling. Coach DreamCoach walks into the games equipment room and comes out with a smaller set of pads for Simon. He hands them to Simon with a smile and says, "Now remember, Simon, size doesn't always mean an advantage so use your dreamy talents out there." He looks up at the rest of the players from all the teams and says, "The first game will be between the Musical Dream Team and the Science Annihilators. The rest of you get changed and back in the stands until your game which could be any one of the following Fridays." Both teams file out into the playing field and get into position for the signal to begin the game. Simon looks at how far he has to jump. There's a distance of a meter between each of the ten trampolines. Every trampoline on the right is dressed in his team's colors while the five on the left are dressed in the opposing team's colors of silver and navy blue. He waits patiently on the far right trampoline with his miniature club in his hand when he hears, "Bang, Bang!" A gun shot into the air and King DreamRoyal yells, "The game begins now!"

Simon starts to bounce on the trampoline just like his fellow team mate Jonas Dreamsound who's located on the opposite far side trampoline. Simon watches as Jonas blocks Rino's first two attempts to score but misses Rino's third attempt and it's ten to nothing for the Science Annihilators. Simon hears the science inclined dreamer crowd cheer as Rino scores second time but Simon sees Brian Dreamery pick up a real ball and hover towards the basket. He throws the balls towards the basket and the hovering disk blocks the ball. Brian catches the same ball as it flies through the air. Simon still hasn't made a move in the game as he tries and figure out what he can do. He sees Brian heading towards the same basket again with the same real ball and throws it towards the basket, Simon quickly jumps from his trampoline onto the opposing team's trampoline and swiftly jumps up from the trampoline and smashes the first disk, the ball goes in and it's now twenty to ten. The music inclined dreamer crowd cheers but briefly as Rino's team mate scores another basket on Simon's side but Simon's not going down without a fight. He jumps onto the nearby opposing team's trampoline, jumps and jumps until the disk is in his sight and he smashes the second one and the crowd cheers and chants, "Simon! Simon! Simon!" Suddenly Simon realizes that the most important players in Dreamator are the dream blockers and not the dream scorers. With this thought, he gets winded as the opposing team's dream blocker attempts to jump him off of their trampoline. Simon flies through the air looking downwards to see where he can land. The crowd gasps at the sight. Simon lands on his stomach on his team's third trampoline knocking the wind out of him again as he tries to get back up without touching the floor. The crowd hushes to see what will be the outcome, Simon stands back up and immediately starts to jump again. The crowd roars for Simon despite the score being fifty to ten for the Science Annihilators. Simon jumps up and blocks Rino's attempt at scoring. Friends off the field but clearly they're not friends during the game as Rino stares him down. Bringing out his competitive nature, Simon just sneers back at Rino as he hovers away to get another real ball but Rino hastily picks up a virtual ball sounding a loud buzzer and the score reflects forty-five to ten. Simon cheers and jumps onto the Science Annihilators third trampoline, jumps and jumps his way to the basket and smashes the third hovering disk just as Nick Daydream scores ten more points for the Musical Dream Team but their mutual excitement's quickly quashed as the dream blocker from the opposing team smashes their first hovering disk. Simon keeps jumping and blocks Rino's attempt to score a second time but Rino has mastered catching the ball as it flies through the air, he quickly comes back and scores. The dream announcer says, "The Science Annihilators have sixty-five points with one smashed hovering disk and the Musical Dream Team have twenty points with three smashed hovering disks." Simon knows what he has to do. He has to smash the last two disks to win the game. Rino yells at his team's dream blockers, "Watch him, push Simon Dreamlee out of the game." Simon jumps on the trampoline and sees the two of them jumping towards him when Jonas Dreamsound jumps in between them throwing them off of their jump trajectory in mid air. He watches as they both struggle to make sure they land on a trampoline and not touch the floor. Simon jumps on the fourth trampoline, jumps and jumps but misses the hovering disk. He waits and re-focuses his jumps to align with the hovering disk. He jumps and successfully smashes the fourth hovering disk. The music inclined dreamers section erupts in cheers. Simon gets catapulted into the air by the opposing team's large dream blocker who jumps onto the same trampoline as him. Simon flies through the air at the height of the dream scorers. He looks down and tries to stop is legs from flopping everywhere in the air. He gains control of his legs as gravity starts to pull him back down towards the game field. He focuses on his own team's third trampoline and lands on it but with that land came a jump through the air again and he uses his small sized to jump two trampoline's over to the far end of his teams side. He jumps in place to regain control over his body. He's now right across from the fifth and final hovering disk. He needs to smash it to win the game. At that moment the dream blocker from the Science Annihilators smashes their second hovering disk. Simon focuses and jumps to the opposing team's trampoline just as Rino scores another ten points for the Science Annihilators. Simon jumps, jumps, aligns himself and jumps up and smashes the fifth and final hovering disk igniting fireworks. With that final smash, the crowds' cheers become deafening the score board reflects seventy-five points for the Science Annihilators to one hundred and seventy for the Musical Dream Team. Simon jumps with his arms in the air and the rest of his team cheers. The Science Annihilators walk off the game field and wait to shake the hands of the winning team once they're done celebrating. The Musical Dream Team walk off the playing field and shake the losing team's hands while they all say, "Good game, good game, really good game, great game." Once Rino has Simon's hand he says, "It was nothing personal you know." Simon says, "I know." Rino says, "You're talented. That was a great game Simon." Simon says, "Thank you. You too Rino, you played a great game." Simon heads into the dressing room and both teams take off their jerseys and padding. The miniature clubs are returned to Coach DreamCoach and they all exit the dressing room to head home for the beginning of the traditional Dreamville weekend summer festival.

Simon and Rino walk out the front door of Dreamtrue School and meet up with Jilla and Almont who stayed behind to walk with them. Jilla says, "That was a great game Rino." Rino says, "Thanks Jilla but I think Simon is the real gamer here." Almont he wants to gloat about their team's win says, "Yup, that's right. Simon's the real gamer. I guess you're not so perfect after all, hey Rino." Rino laughs and says, "Perfect, I've never said that to anyone. But go ahead and brag Almont. Your team won this round but there's still more rounds to come." Rino and Jilla start walking towards the DreamScifi's house. Simon says, "See you Monday or at the summer festival." Jilla says, "Yeah see you." Almont says, "Well I guess we better get our hover boards." They walk towards the hover parkade and get on their hover boards and race to their crossroads. Almont says, "Hey come on give a guy a break here." Simon says, "I can't help it if I always make it here first." Almont says, "Eat more. You need a little weight to hold you back." They look at each other and laugh at Almont's joke. Simon says, "You know, I had a strange dream last night." Almont says, "Oh yeah what about?" Simon asks, "What are you doing tomorrow?" Almont says, "Not much since this summer festival is being entertained by non-musical plays instead of us fellow musicians. Why?" Simon says, "You should come over and I'll play you my dream." Almont says, "Alright dude, that's cool with me. See you at ten-ish, eleven-ish." Simon says, "Cool, see you then." Almont hovers off in the direction of his house and Simon hovers towards his house.

Hovering along his hover way driveway, he stares at the DreamRoyal castle. He lowers his hover board down onto the solar panel grid and walks into his house. He walks into the kitchen through the back door and sees his father sitting in his usual spot waiting for supper. Mr. Dreamlee says, "Oh hey son. Come and sit. I made supper tonight for us. It's called Apple Crumb with cinnamon." Simon looks around and asks, "Where's mom?" He takes a bite of his supper while he awaits his father's answer. Simon's dad says, "She's working late to make her latest fashion line dream come true for its début tomorrow morning. It'll be a happy Saturday for your mother. Is there anything you want to share with me?" Simon puts some vanilla ice cream on his apple crumb and says, "No, not really. Should I have something to say to you?" Mr. Dreamlee smiles at Simon and says, "Virtual news replay." The hovering virtual newscaster starts to post images of Simon playing Dreamator and his best moments during the game. The media clown says, "Dreamily Simon Dreamlee, smallest Dreamator player ever shown here smashing the fifth and final hovering disk to win the game for the Musical Dream Team today has earned the nick name of the gamer. Way to go Simon Dreamlee. Keep dreaming and dreams do become true Dreamville." Simon looks at his father who says, "Virtual news off." Mr. Dreamlee turns to his son and says, "I'm proud of you son. Looks like you have your mother's gift for Dreamator. She was also a dream blocker and a really good one too." Simon asks, "Why didn't she ever talk to me about Dreamator?" Mr. Dreamlee replies, "Well son, Dreamator was banned at the profoundly cruel request of Principal Toombs eleven years ago but since King DreamRoyal is now back to his usual self all Dreamvillians including him want to reinstate the Town's game. Today son you did a great job at bringing everyone together in the spirit of good dreams don't ever really get banished." Simon says, "Well, I got winded a few times during the game so I want to get some early dreamy zees tonight. But, before I go upstairs dad is there anything that you want to share with me?" Mr. Dreamlee says, "Actually yes there is. I have a new invention. Well, it's not new really, more innovative though." Mr. Dreamlee pulls out a regular hover board and shows it to Simon. Simon looks at it and shrugs his shoulders. Mr. Dreamlee puts the hover board on the floors and says, "Hover." The board starts hovering at the command of his voice. Simon's eyes get big and round, he says, "Voice commanded hover boards. Dad this is awesome!" Mr. Dreamlee says, "I'm happy you like it son now watch this. Hover board, come to me." The hover board goes to Mr. Dreamlee. Simon smiles and looks at his dad. Mr. Dreamlee says, "Like my invention for voice activated hand held computers, the hover boards will only recognize the owners voice, therefore, it will only follow its owners command." Simon says, "Great. That is so great. I want one as soon as they're available." Simon's dad smiles and says, "Son, don't you know me by now. This one right here is yours. Now, when you take it out of its wrapping, place your fingers in the indentations underneath and start to record commands based on the instructions and it's all yours." Simon says, "Oh thank you dad. Thank you so much." Mr. Dreamlee says, "Ah… it's the least I can do for you. This is marketed tomorrow and everyone will have one by Monday. Have fun son." Simon runs upstairs into his bedroom with his new, innovative, voice activated hover board.

Simon closes the door to his bedroom, rips the wrapping around his new hover board and is excited by his shiny red and purple hover board. He finds the list of commands to program into the hover board. He flips the board over and places his finger prints in the indentations and one by one says the commands. Simon says, "Hover, hover to me, hover right, hover left, hover up, hover down, cease hover mode, still hover mode, hover to solar panel grid, hover fast, hover slow, manual hover mode." Simon removes his finger prints and places the board on his bed and says, "Hover." The board hovers. Simon says, "Hover to me." The hover board hovers to him. Simon says, "Cease hover mode." The hover board hovers down onto the floor. Simon brings his board outside and removes his old hover board and says, "Hover to solar panel grid." The new hover board hovers onto the solar panel grid. Simon smiles and brings his first hover board with him into the house and goes back up into his bedroom. He decides he'll keep his old hover board for awhile before sending it down the obsolete technology recycling chute. Boomboom Booya runs into his room and jumps on Simon's bed "woof". Frankie Noodles sits in the doorway, "Meow, meow, meow." Simon spent the whole night programming his new hover board, with this occupying his time; he didn't realize the time was getting late. Simon says, "Whoa, sure is dark outside and I didn't even notice." He closes his bedroom door and attaches his dream catcher to his head. He puts his head on his pillow and starts to dream. He doesn't dream about anything different than he had the night before, in fact, he dreams about the exact same scenario with King DreamRoyal the third, the queen, his servants and the gargoyles living in the outside world. He still feels like he's besides the ancient king and they both peer out through the looking window and that same terribly cruel song resounds in his head during his dream.

Chapter Three – Evil Returns To Dreamville

Saturday morning, exactly one week until King DreamRoyal and Miss LossDream's wedding. Simon wakes up when Boomboom Booya jumps on him scaring Frankie Noodles who screeches as she jumps off the bed. "Meow…" Simon says, "Happy Saturday Boomboom Booya and Frankie Noodles." He detaches the dream catcher from his head this time with the intention of viewing his dream when he gets downstairs. Simon gets out of bed and stands in front of his window that faces the backyard. He puts his computer chip sized hand held computer in his pocket just as a tiny pebble hits him in the forehead. Simon exclaims, "Ouch… hey…" He looks out his window to see who's the prankster and sees a very frustrated Almont. Almont says, "It's about time you wake up. My virtual watch says eleven thirty and I've been here since ten thirty, o'clock. Why'd I say that? Why o'clock?" Simon holds his forehead and says, "Why'd you do that? Throw a rock at my forehead." Almont says, "I wasn't aiming to hit you but it got your attention didn't it. Now let me in already." Simon says, "Just knock, my parents will let you inside." Almont replies, "Your parents passed me on my way here, probably, on their way to the summer festivities." Simon says, "Alright, I'll be downstairs in two minutes. Oh I've got something really cool to show you." Simon runs downstairs through the foyer, through the kitchen while Almont does his hover board tricks in the Dreamlee's backyard. Simon opens the back door and meets Almont outside. Simon says, "Do that again!" Almont standing on his hover board flips the board under his feet and lands back on his hover board once it's done a full revolution. Simon says, "Awesome!" Almont laughs and says, "Ha-ha. Yeah, I worked every day on this trick from the first day I got my hover board." Simon says, "And you're only showing me now." Almont says, "Well… It's nothing that special besides the Dreamator dream scorers have tricks that blow me out of contention. I guess you didn't really notice seeing how you concentrated on your dream blocker position." Simon says, "Yeah, I guess." Almont says, "Well what's so cool that you have to show me?" Almont opens the back door to go inside Simon's house. Simon says, "Where are you going?" Almont replies, "Inside to view your quote, strange, unquote, dream, you said you wanted me to view today. That's why you invited me over here isn't it?" Simon says, "Yes but I have two things now and the first thing I want to show you is out here." Almont closes the door and follows Simon passed Wendy the cow and her robot caretaker to Simon's hover board and hover bike stand. Almont says, "Alright what's going on?" Simon says, "Take a look." Almont looks at Simon's hover board and excitedly says, "Oh wow, what an awesome paint job. Where'd you get it done or did you do it?" Simon says, "No but watch." Perplexed, Almont looks at Simon as he says, "Hover." Surprised, Almont quickly steps back as the hover board begins to hover. Simon says, "Hover to me." Simon's hover board hovers to him. Almont exclaims, "Voice recognition! Awesome! Is this another one of your father's inventions and when can I get one in at the Dreamville mall?" Simon says, "Cease hover mode." They, both, watch as the hover board makes its way back to the solar panel grid, lowers itself down and ceases to hover. Almont says, "Wow!" Simon says, "Come on, now I have my strange dream I want you to view." Not wanting to take his eyes off of the new hover board, Almont walks backwards towards Simon's back door. Simon pulls him inside and shuts the door.

They walk through the kitchen into the virtual room. Almont takes a seat and asks, "I'll be able to get one of those voice recognition hover boards won't I?" Simon replies, "Yes, today in fact." Almont exclaims, "Right on!" Simon says, "Viadream awaken please." Viadream yawning as usual appears on the virtual screen and says, "Simon Dreamlee, long time, no see. What can I play for you today?" Simon takes his computer chip sized hand held computer and inserts it in the pod. Simon says, "Viadream please play my latest dream." Viadream replies, "With dreamy pleasure." Simon's musical dream, although more of a play, starts to materialize on the virtual, three dimensional, screen. Almont is immediately pulled into the story. They both watch and listen intently to the story unfold before their eyes. Almont takes mental note of the text about the gargoyles and the exiled MagicDream family. Almont is clearly not enthused by the evil, confused and poorly informed Outsiders song regarding the gargoyles. Simon's dream ends and Viadream reappears. She says, "Great dream Simon, a very great mystery for you to solve. Will that be all for today?" Simon says, "Yes, thank you Viadream, that will be all for today." Viadream starts to yawn and stretch her tiny little limbs as she disappears and the virtual dream player shuts off. Simon turns to Almont and waits for a response. Almont just stares back at him. Simon asks, "Well… What do you think?" Almont replies, "Didn't King DreamRoyal mention something about a legend." Simon says, "Yes." Almont says, "Aren't legends usually myths." Simon says, "Yes, I think so." Almont says, "I think your dream is just a fictional dream and like the love story you dreamt about over a year ago, you'll dream about the happy ending." Simon replies, "Yeah okay. Maybe you're right. It's still a strange dream though." Almont nods his head in agreement and says, "Sure is a weird one." Simon and Almont sit on the couch as the hovering clock hovers by indicating the time is twelve forty-five in the afternoon. Almont says, "Well what now?" Simon says, "I'm hungry, I think there's some lemon meringue tarts in the fridge." They go into the kitchen to enjoy their lunch. Suddenly, Simon's virtual communicator goes off and his Dreamator team captain, Brian Dreamery says, "Simon?" Simon says, "I'm here Brian. What is it?" Brian says, "Happy Saturday to you. I know this is very short notice but we need you to come down to the dream coliseum right now." Simon says, "Now, why now?" Brian says, "It's the only time slot our team can get to practice Dreamator. It's important that you make it today because we play again next Friday against the sports inclined Dreamers." Simon says, "Yeah, alright then I'll be there. Give me fifteen minutes." Brian says, "Great, communication out." Simon looks at Almont; Almont swallows his last bit of lemon meringue tart, Simon says, "Sorry, I guess I have to cut this visit short." Almont says, "Ah whatever, I'll sit in the stands while you practice and afterwards we can go to my house to play some virtual three dimensional video games, Virtual Dreamator." Simon says, "Great. Well we should get going." They head into the backyard from the back door and get on their hover boards. "Simon says, "Hover. Hover forward, hover right. Hover fast." And they're on their way, hovering down Dreamway Street when they reach their crossroads, Simon says, "Hover Right." He forgets to command his hover board to slow down and as the hover board turns onto AppleDreams Street, Simon goes flying through the air. Simon yells, "Ah…." Almont starts laughing as Simon tumbles on the ground, "Ha-ha… Are you alright?" Simon yells, "Cease hover mode." His voice recognition activated hover board promptly drops to the ground. Simon continues to say with a laugh, "I'm fine. Ha-ha." Almont hovers to Simon and extends his hand to help him up. Simon walks to his hover board and checks it to make sure there's no cracks or breaks. Simon says, "Looks fine." Almont says, "Yeah well your knee doesn't look so fine." Simon looks down at his right knee and sees he's got a scrape and is slightly bleeding. He looks up at Almont and says, "Looks like I need a little practice with my new board. Ha-ha." Almont smiles and says, "Well great you're okay. Let's get to your Dreamator practice." Simon steps on his hover board and says, "Hover, hover forward, hover fast." They hover straight towards DreamHappy Street. Simon says, "Slow hover. Hover left." They hover into the hover parkade and Simon says, "Cease hover mode." His hover board hovers into the solar panel grid and stops hovering. Almont comes up behind him and parks his hover board. Almont says, "Well you still beat me here even with your little spill back there." Simon and Almont high five each other and walk into Dreamtrue School.

In the corridor, Simon walks in front of the principal's office and looks in the trophy case. He sees his mother's name engraved on one of the multiple gold plaques under her maiden name. Almont asks, "What?" Simon replies, "My mother's name on the golden plaque on the Dreamator trophy. See right there, Mirabélla FashiDream, of course, before she became Mrs. Dreamlee." Almont says, "Wow, your mom was a talented Dreamator dream blocker just like Miss LossDream mentioned." Simon says, "Yeah. I just hope that I don't disappoint her by being a mediocre Dreamator dream blocker." Almont says, "Are you kidding? Simon you're awesome!" Simon says, "That was just one game. What if all it was; was beginners luck?" Almont says, "Come on gamer, get to your practice and quit doubting yourself." Almont smiles, grabs Simon's arm by his small, slender bicep and directs him towards the doors to the Dreamville dream coliseum. They enter the playing field and meet up with Brian Dreamery. Brian says, "Hey Dreamlee. Are you ready to practice Simon?" Simon says, "I sure am." Brian turns to Almont and says, "What are you doing here Almont?" Almont replies, "Oh I just came to watch." Brian says, "Well I'm sorry but I only have passes for our Dreamator team members. You'll have to leave or wait outside of Dreamtrue School." Simon looks at Almont, Almont says, "That's cool, I want to go buy my new voice recognition hover board anyway. Simon I'll catch up with you later dude." Simon says, "Yeah later." Brian says, "Again sorry Almont." Almont runs towards the exit doors and yells back, "Don't sweat it, really not a big deal." Almont exits the coliseum. Simon and Brian get into their positions with the rest of the team members. Brian says, "Mostly, what we need to do is strategize and create game plans based on what we anticipate as possible game scenarios and designate a task to each player." Brian hovers up with the other two dream scorers. Brian says, "The dream scorers will test out our new voice recognition hover boards." Simon and Jonas watch as at first, they take spills similar to Simon's earlier one but eventually, quickly and competently master their maneuvers. Brian even tested out a situation where he's high in the sky and missteps on his hover board. Falling he yells, "Hover to me." His hover board hovers under him, catches him and he stands back up on the board. Everyone cheers and claps. Hughes Dreamy and Nick Daydream practice the same maneuvers as their team captain. Simon turns to Jonas and says, "We should practice controlling our bodies while we jump from trampoline to trampoline and practice aligning ourselves to shatter the hovering disks." Brian, Hughes and Nick observe the dream blockers. Brian says, "Simon is clearly the better calculator." Brian continues to say, "In the end, I think we all decide that Simon Dreamlee's the designated shatterer while Jonas Dreamsound concentrates on blocking the opponent's balls." Simon says, "But he will step in only if absolutely necessary and vice versa. Agreed?" Everyone replies simultaneously, "Agreed!" Hughes says, "Maybe we should have some kind of team song or chant?" Brian says, "That's a great idea. Anything you have in mind Hughes." Hughes hesitates but says, "As the Musical Dream Team we beam, we'll score, block and shatter. Our game is mean but clean. Go Musical Dream Team." Simon says, "I like it." Brian, Nick and Jonas nod their heads to show they agree and all together say, "Cool!" Brian looks at the hovering clock and says, "Two thirty, great practice guys but our times up." Just as he finishes his sentence the sports inclined dreamers walk into the playing field with their team jerseys of green and gold. Simon reads their team name; Sportanators. Their extremely large, tall and muscular team captain yells at Brian, "Brian your times up. I hope you dreamt up some music to put your fans to sleep so they don't witness us slaughtering you Friday." Brian replies, "The playing fields all yours Tito." Brian, Nick and Hughes say, "Hover down. Cease hover mode." They get off of their hover boards and as a team they walk out of the dream coliseum. Simon asks, "Who is that?" Brian says, "Tito MuscleDream, don't let him get to you. He just likes to try and get under your skin or in your head." They all walk out of Dreamtrue School, the dream scorers get on their hover boards and voice command them to hover. Brian says, "See you guys in class on Monday." Simon says, "Monday." Jonas says, "See you guys" as he gets into his parents hover car. Simon finds himself alone in front of Dreamtrue School when his personal virtual communicator starts to stream a breaking virtual newscast.

Simon watches the virtualcast. The field media news clown asks, "King DreamRoyal when did you notice, your prized gargoyle was missing?" King DreamRoyal with Miss LossDream by his side replies, "Well, I actually noticed early this morning but I didn't report it to authorities until now." The media clown asks, "Which gargoyle is it?" King DreamRoyal replies, "The tall, stately male lion. According to my family history, King Régimand DreamRoyal the third named him Gargantua." The media clown asks, "Who or what do you think happened to this Gargantua. Who do you think stole him and why?" King DreamRoyal who clearly looks distressed replies, "I have no idea. I don't know. As far as I was aware all evil was already banished from Dreamville but apparently not." The media desk clown comes on virtual air and says, "So there we have it fellow Dreamvillians, King Régimand DreamRoyal the tenth has yet another caper and dilemma to try and solve. We'll all be watching. Try and have a dreamy Dreamville day Dreamvillians." Simon's virtualcast shuts off as the breaking update's complete. Simon puts his virtual communicator in his pocket. Simon says to himself, "Who's Gargantua? My dreams, Gargantua! Why do I have this nagging feeling in the pit of my stomach that I know this name?" Simon shakes off his nagging intuition and yells, "Hover to me." His hover board rises from the solar panel grid in the hover parkade and hovers towards Simon. Simon says, "Still Hover mode." He gets on his hover board and says, "Hover forward." Up the street to his crossroad and he commands, "Hover left." He slowly hovers home. Once at the end of his hover driveway, he says, "Still hover." He hovers in the air while he looks up at King DreamRoyal's castle. The nagging feeling just won't leave him alone. Simon says, "I feel like I should know something. But, what is it?" He's confused, perplexed and clueless but intrigued and astounded that such an occurrence could again take place in Dreamville. Simon says, "Could Miss DreamNot and the Dream squad chief be back and if so how?" He hears his dog barking in the backyard, Woof, woof..." His dog, Boomboom Booya's barking noise distracts him from his personal thoughts and Simon says, "Hover left." He hovers into the back yard and he says, "Cease hover." His board hovers into the solar panel grid and Simon hops off. Simon says, "Cool! I don't have to say the full command after all." Boomboom Booya jumps on Simon and knocks him to the ground. Simon says, "Down girl, down Boomboom Booya." Simon manages to get back to his feet and says, "Boomboom Booya have you been teasing the cow, Wendy, again? Now, you know how much she hates that." Boomboom Booya barks, "Woof." Simon laughs and says, "Alright, come on girl, inside." Simon opens the backdoor to the kitchen and Boomboom Booya runs inside followed by Simon.

Alone, at three in the afternoon, Simon stands in the kitchen playing with his dog and his cat, when he hears banging in the front of the house. He hears his parents hover car pull up into the hover car garage. They walk into the house talking with distress in their voices. Mirabélla Dreamlee walks into the kitchen and immediately breathes a sigh of relief when she sees Simon. She says, "Charles he's here." Mr. Dreamlee walks in the kitchen and says, "Oh good. Son with what just happened we were worried about you." Simon says, "I'm fine. It's terrible that someone stole King DreamRoyal's gargoyle." His parents look at him silently. Simon says, "Do the dream squads cops think that Miss DreamNot and the ex dream squad chief are back to cause chaos?" Mr. Dreamlee says, "We don't know son. Please go to your room." Simon says, "May I go to the attic?" Mrs. Dreamlee says, "Go ahead. I'll call you down for supper." Simon quickly goes up both flights of stairs and into the attic. He begins to observe all of Dreamville as the summer festivities are interrupted by the unforeseen theft of the gargoyle. He turns his attention to King DreamRoyal's castle, particularly, the spot where the missing gargoyle stood in a proud statuesque pose. He looks at each gargoyle carefully and compares his notes from two days ago. Simon carefully observes every miniscule detail and says to himself, "The female lion, two nights ago, faced the front door and today she faces the front window. The two monkeys faced the blue bells two days ago and today they face each other. That's strange? The two dogs faced the sunflowers two days ago and today they face the two snakes and the two snakes face the two dogs today when two days ago they faced the fence. What's going on? The two goats are facing the apple orchard today and two days ago they were also facing the apple orchard. The two wolves face the missing gargoyles usual spot today while two days ago they faced the two goats. Oh my dreams, these gargoyles either really move around but that's ridiculous or there's another sinister plot being perpetrated in Dreamville by someone." An hour goes by while Simon takes notation of his observations from today and the past couple of days. Simon says, "Me and anyone who read my notes cannot deny that these supposedly free standing rock statues do move because they not only shift where they face but their arms, feet even eyes shift around too. The legend must be true and if it is then the missing gargoyle, Gargantua, must still be in

Dreamville somewhere." As soon as he's done thinking out loud, his virtual communicator goes off and Almont's tiny virtual image beams in front of Simon's eyes. Almont says, "Come in Simon." Simon says, "I'm here Almont." Almont says, "Simon did you hear the bad news?" Simon says, "Yes, I heard about the missing gargoyle, Gargantua." Almont has tears in his eyes and says, "You haven't heard, have you?" Simon says, "Heard what? Why are you crying?" Almont wipes his cheeks and says, "Jilla's been kidnapped." Simon says, "What?" Almont says, "Apparently, Rino was the last to see her after they broke up at his place last night. Dumb smooching Rino has a new girlfriend, of course, she's more appropriate for him, a sixteen year old name Dee FictiveDream." Simon says, "Okay back to Jilla." Almont says, "Yeah, she never made it home last night and her parents reported her missing this morning but the dream squad chief wanted to give her the day to go home but she's still not home and no one can find her anywhere." Simon says, "Oh my dreams. Is Rino in jail?" Almont says, "No, apparently Dee was there in his living room when he broke up with Jilla so he has an alibi." Simon says, "She must have a broken heart. Do you think she ran away into the Outsiders world?" Almont says, "Never, she probably would have moped about him for a couple days but she'd never run away. Her parents think so too." Simon asks, "How do you know?" Almont replies, "Our parents are close friends. Seriously Simon, Jilla has been kidnapped. We have to find her." Simon hears his mother as she says, "Simon suppertime." Almont says, "It's okay, go eat. If you can eat, I can't." Simon says, "I'll virtual communicate with you in twenty minutes. I have important notations to show you." Almont sniffles and says, "Alright. Terminate communication." Like that, Almont was gone and Simon's virtual communicator turns itself off. Simon rushes down both flights of stairs and into the newly updated kitchen.

Once in the newly renovated kitchen, Simon's confronted by his parents and the new female dream squad chief. The dream squad chief says, "Simon there's no need to be alarmed. I'm here because one of your close friends is missing." Simon quickly says, "Jilla, I know. Almont just virtually told me." She says, "Okay and I know how shockingly un-dreamily hard this news must be for you to hear." Simon says, "Oh my dreams, nightmares. Indeed, very surprised because Jilla is not the type to run away." The dream squad chief continues to say, "That answered one of my questions. Now, you know her on a personal level. Do you think she could simply be hiding because of her ex-boyfriend?" Simon replies, "No, she would probably mope a little but still hang out with Almont and I. That's more her character. Besides she'd eventually realize that he's too old for her." The dream squad chief asks, "Do you think she's been kidnapped?" Simon replies, "Without a doubt in my mind. I don't know anyone who would want to harm her except for Miss DreamNot and maybe the ex dream squad chief." The dream squad chief says, "Okay, thank you. That will be all." Simon asks, "Do you have a suspect?" The dream squad chief says, "No, not yet." Simon says, "Can I suggest Miss DreamNot." The dream squad chief replies, "It's not her Simon, we have invisible hovering video surveillance all around her shack in the woods and she's been there the whole time. Even the ex dream squad chief is on video." Mr. Dreamlee says, "Okay, I guess we're done here. Thank you so much for coming by Miss dream squad chief." He walks her to the front door and she leaves the premises. Simon's mom gives him a hug and says, "They'll find her Simon, don't you worry." Simon says, "I'm not hungry. I think I'm just going to go upstairs." Mrs. Dreamlee releases her grip on her boy and Simon walks out of the kitchen. Once he's just outside of the doorway, he overhears his mother and father talking when Mr. Dreamlee walks in the kitchen and says, "I hope things work out positively and they find Jilla alive." Mrs. Dreamlee says, "What if it's worse like she's been taken to the Outside world?" Mr. Dreamlee says, "Then every Dreamvillians worse fear would be realized; the Outsiders know where we are and found a way inside to terrorize us. Hopefully this isn't the beginning of the end of dreams come true." With that last uttered thought from his father's mouth, Simon quietly runs upstairs to the attic.

That same Saturday, Simon sits in his parent's attic and re-reads all his increasingly disturbing notations. Simon says, "Why did King DreamRoyal tell me about their legend? There has to be a reason." Simon takes out his virtual communicator and contacts Almont. Simon says, "Almont come in." Almont's virtual image appears before him and he replies, "I'm here Simon. Thanks for virtually communicating back with me." Simon says, "Almont I have a theory." Almont asks, "What's your theory?" Simon says, "You're going to think I'm crazy but just hear me out." Almont replies, "Alright, I'm listening." Simon continues to say, "I've been surveying the gargoyles on DreamRoyal hill ever since King DreamRoyal told us about their legend. Now, at first, there wasn't much to note but there were still little things, like shifting of their eyes gazes from one day to the next that suggested to me that they do, in fact, come alive at night. Of course, I know this isn't remotely enough evidence to prove that they do, in fact, come alive at night. However, lately during this past week, those little details have majorly increased and the biggest discovery I've made is today all the statues are not facing where they usually face. They've moved completely." Almont refrains from commentating on what Simon just revealed as his new pastime but still says, "Simon, I think you have too much time on your hands. I think your being the Dreamator dream blocker will be excellent for you and your overactive, insatiable mind's imagination." Simon says, "I'm not being ridiculous Almont. I'm serious Almont. The gargoyle statues have moved completely. Please, you have to believe me. Remember a year ago and my dream then, well, my latest dream that I let you preview, well, I think it has something to do with what's happened to Jilla." Almont says, "Wait a minute, a few seconds ago this was about gargoyles and there was no mention of Jilla's disappearance." Simon realizes how absurd he sounds and decides to lie and says, "Maybe I'm not making myself clear. I think that Miss DreamNot has managed to find a way to move the gargoyles and kidnapped Jilla. You see moving the gargoyles and even taking one of them makes everyone think that the gargoyles really do come alive at night." Almont says, "That makes sense. How will we ever know for sure and catch her?" Simon says, "I don't know yet. I have to think about that." Almont's mother opens his bedroom door and says, "Time for bed Almont. Sweet Dreams." Almont says to his mother, "Sweet dreams mom." Almont turns to Simon and says, "I've got to go. Talk to you tomorrow. Sweet dreams Simon." Simon says, "Oh yeah sure Almont. Sweet dreams Almont." Before signing off, Almont says, "I'm sleeping with my window shut and locked tonight. I think that you should too. Oh and don't talk to any media clowns." Simon says, "Right. Sign off." His virtual communicator shuts off. Simon looks around the attic and walks up to his new hovering telescope. He grabs it and looks through it at the gargoyles as the night keeps falling over Dreamville. Simon says, "They're not moving yet." He hears his mother coming up the attic steps, once in the attic, she says, "Simon, sweetheart, time for bed." Simon releases his hovering telescope and follows her downstairs to the second level. He goes in his bedroom and turns around to face his mother. She says, "Sweet dreams son." She closes his bedroom door. Simon sits on his bed contemplating what he should do. He says to himself, "Should I stay up to prove that they do, in fact, come alive at night or should I fall asleep and see what I will dream? Either way, I need concrete proof or I'll just be ridiculed, a laughing stock for Dreamvillians." The hovering clock hovers passed him indicating the time to be ten thirty-five at night. He gets up to let the hovering clock out of his room, the clock hovers out into the hallway and then he shuts the door. Simon walks back to his bed, sits, attaches his dream catcher to his head and puts his head on his hands on his pillow. His virtual communicator turns on and Almont appears. He says, "Pssst… Simon? Simon, are you awake?" Simon sits up and responds, "Yes Almont, I'm awake." Almont says, "I think we should look into the matter of the existence of the ancient text you dreamed about." Simon says, "Meet me at the paper book library tomorrow at ten in the morning." Almont says, "Okay see you then. Sign off." Simon kept his window open, he can hear the dream squad cops patrolling all of Dreamville in hopes of finding Jilla and he says to himself, "Tonight, I'll sneak out and document the gargoyles transformation from statues to living, breathing, intelligent creatures." Accidentally, Simon puts his head on his pillow. Instantaneously, he falls to sleep and starts his dream.

Monkey, stupid and ugly monkey,
They are nature gone awry to punish humans for their sins.
Monkeys are the living deadly sin of sloth.
Burn, burn, burn and be gone.

Burn, burn, burn and be gone.
Burn, burn, burn and be gone.
Burn, burn, burn and be gone.
Burn, burn, burn and be gone.

Simon's dream begins where the first one ended with the faint sound of the cruel song sung by the multiple Outsiders over and over again. The song becomes distant and fades to no longer be heard just as three faces flash. The faces are of King Régimand DreamRoyal the third and his trusted servants, Timatie and Milany but they seem transparent like ghosts rather than solid beings. Simon's dream becomes less historical and more theatrical as a stage slowly forms and suddenly three dancers appear. They portray the three aforementioned characters. There are spectators along the stage who eagerly watch as the dancers prance through the stage of underground passageways and through tunnels. The three are running along with fourteen shadowy black creatures with wings, the gargoyles. The cruel song re-begins by the sudden apparition of multiplying Outsiders portrayed by a large group of dancers dressed in peasants clothing. They dance frantically around the three Dreamvillians and the fourteen gargoyles. Within seconds, sounds of screeches are heard by all as the mob captures; beats and almost kills one of the dancer's portraying a Dreamvillian, particularly, King DreamRoyal the third. A dancer dressed in white garbs dances onto the stage and into the large group of Outsiders and appears to be offering himself in exchange for the life of the King. They release the King who runs into the Dreamville tunnel. The fourteen large shadowy figures and the three Dreamvillians dance around to portray their terror. The fourteen big shadowy figures start to dance strongly; they come together and push a rock over the opening closing and blocking the entrance into the underground Dreamvillian tunnels. The mob of Outsiders is powerless to get into the tunnels. His dream fills with darkness, he feels cramped in a narrow space and a girl's face flashes, it could be Jilla's face but the flash is really quick. The gargoyle made in the image of a male lion stands over her, like he's guarding her but also like he's a prisoner himself. The stage becomes light, grey and smog filled as the image of an Outsiders brick city becomes the new background to Simon's dream. Suddenly, his dream fills with a conversation between two invisible female voices. One female says, "I sure hope Gargantua's right about this boy, Lionessa." Lionessa replies, "Wolverina, I don't doubt him at all. Gargantua's convinced this boy's the key to help us." On the stage, the same little boy from his dream of over a year ago flashes with the key around his neck and a song.

Truth dreamer, truth dreamer
Believe what you dream.
Although, confusing it may be.
Find her.
Find them all.
Taken by influential Outsider,
Kidnapped by the night creature but not yet harmed.
Truth dreamer, truth dreamer
Do your research.
Find her.
Save her.
Save them.
Save all.
Truth dreamer, truth dreamer
He took her to them.
Monday, he'll, another creature will, take two more to them.
They mean no harm.
But they could turn.

If they do not get what they want,
Freedom to be
Freedom to love
Freedom for the others,
Just like you.
Remember truth dreamer,
They mean no harm.
They just want to be saved too.
Truth dreamer, truth dreamer
Dreamville's secret residents
Need you.
Bring them their daylight gems.

Chapter Four – The Ancient Text Of Master MagicDream

Early Sunday morning, Simon's virtual communicator goes off and Rino DreamScifi's virtual image streams in front of Simon's just awakening eyes. Rino says, "Simon, come in." Simon sits up, detaches his dream catcher from his head and in typical Dreamvillian cursing fashion, he exclaims, "Oh my un-dreamy dreams!" Rino says, "What?" Simon replies, "Yes, Rino, I'm here. Why are you virtually communicating with me? Seriously, what do you want?" Rino says, "I know this seems odd and all but even though my feelings for Jilla have changed, I still consider her a friend. I know that you and Almont aren't going to just let the dream squad cops screw up and never find her." Simon says, "Why would you think they'll screw up?" Rino replies, "Because the new female dream squad chief is the original dream squad chief's daughter." Simon says, "What? How can that be? " Rino says, "I overheard my father talking to my mother last night before I went to bed and he said that Miss DreamNot and the ex dream squad chief were teenaged lovers, of course, taboo, and they had a daughter. Miss DreamNot rejected the dream squad chief's marriage proposal, we all know now why and their child was raised by the dream squad chief's parents as his baby sister, although, they later told her who are her real parents, she forgave them both so no one even needed to be made aware of the un-dreamy, non-Dreamvillian, family situation but it turns out everyone knew. That is, all the adults know." Simon says, "Teenaged parents. That's way too young but just because of who her father and mother are, doesn't mean she'll be a bad dream squad chief. However, Rino, you're right about Almont and me. Meet us at the paper book library at ten this morning." Clearly relieved, Rino says, "Thank you Simon. Thank you so much. I really, truly, want to find Jilla and make sure she's okay." Simon says, "Ah Rino…" Rino says, "What?" Simon replies, "Don't bring her, you know, Dee FictiveDream." Rino says, "Of course not, I'm not looking to commit genocide and eliminating everyone including myself." Simon doesn't laugh at the science inclined dreamer's attempted joke and says, "Oh and I can't control how Almont will react and treat you either. He's well rather fond of Jilla." Rino says, "I'll be there regardless. Sign out." Rino's gone, Simon's virtual communicator is shut off and he looks around his room and says to himself, "Oh my un-dreamy dreams, I really should've stayed up last night." He gets out of bed and opens his bedroom door. The hovering clock hovers by indicating the time as eight forty-five Sunday morning. Boomboom Booya jumps off of Simon's bed and stretches her limbs while Frankie Noodles rubs against his legs for attention. Simon bends over and pets his female feline. He sees that his parents are already up and hears them down in the virtual viewing room reviewing their latest dreams come true. He walks back into his room and puts his computer chip sized, hand held computer in his pocket. He walks out and into the bathroom. He brushes his teeth and says, "Well I wonder what today will bring." He rinses his mouth with mouthwash and says, "I'll floss later." He walks out of the bathroom and downstairs to the first level.

He walks into the kitchen and grabs a chocolate muffin for breakfast. His mother walks in the kitchen and says, "Simon dear, you're up early for a Sunday, summer festival day." Simon turns around to face his mother and replies, "Yeah, I'm thinking of going to the paper book library and doing some really ancient school research." Mrs. Dreamlee says, "Sure son, whatever you need to do to take your mind off of, I mean, to stimulate your mind." Simon says, "Happy Sunday Mom." As he walks out the back door and into the backyard, he finishes chewing the last bite of his chocolate muffin and says, "Hover to me." His hover board hovers to him and waits for the next command. Simon watches the back alley as one of the many dream squad cops hovering squad cars hovers by his house's backyard. This startles the cow, Wendy, "Moo… Moo…. Moo…" Simon says to Wendy, the cow, "Girl, it'll be okay. It's okay." Mr. Dreamlee opens the back door and says, "What's going on back here?" Simon replies, "Nothing dad, Wendy, the cow, was scared by the hover squad car that hovered by in the back alley." Mr. Dreamlee says, "Oh my dreams, hey, well, she'll be okay. Try to have a happy Sunday Simon." He shuts the door. Simon gets on his hovering board and says, "Hover forward." He hovers up his hover driveway and says, "Hover right." He hovers down his street and straight onto Almont's drive and past his house. Simon can see that Almont's hover board is gone. Simon says to himself, "He must already be there. Oh my un-dreamy dreams, I have to get there before Rino does. Fast hover." His hover board picks up speed. He comes to the turn off onto AncientDreams Street and he says, "Slow Hover. Hover right. Fast Hover" Simon arrives at the Paper Book Library and says, "Slow hover. Still hover. Cease hover." He leaves his hover board by the steps of the front entrance. He looks around for Almont he sees his hover board but not Almont. Almont comes around the corner of the building and says, "It's about time you get here." Simon says, "Sorry, I got sidetracked by my startled cow when a dream squad cop car hovered by in the back alley." Almont says, "Well, we should go in then. Who knows how many books we have to read before finding the right one?" Simon hesitates and says, "Just a moment as he sees Rino hovering up to the paperback library. Almont sees his friends eyes are fixed on something behind him so he turns around. Almont says, "How dare he show his face around Dreamville so soon." Rino says, "Hover still. Cease hover." He steps off of his hover board and says, "Well I made it here Simon." Almont turns to Simon and says, "What? You knew he was coming?" Simon says, "Look Almont he feels bad about his unexpected change of feelings but he wants to help Jilla and face it, we'll need all the help we can get." Rino walks up to them and looks at Almont. Almont turns around and face to face with Rino, he says, "Rino, you were never good enough for Jilla anyway, not to mention, you were too old for her too. I should have half a mind to punch you out but that wouldn't be very Dreamvillian of me, would it?" Rino nods his head in agreement and they start up the steps into the paperback book library when Almont turns and hits Rino with his fist. Rino falls on the cement steps. Simon says, "Almont, you ancient brute. This is not time to let your feeling interfere with the process of finding clues to save Jilla." Rino gets up and pushes Almont onto the steps. Simon says, "Rino no, don't reciprocate." Almont gets up, Simon steps in between the two large boys and says, "If you're going to fight then you'll have to fight through me." Almont puffs up and says, "This isn't your fight Simon." Rino puffs up and says, "That's right so step out of the way." Simon yells, "ALMONT ALLDREAM, RINO DREAMSCIFI; DO YOU THINK JILLA MUSIDREAM WOULD APPROVE OF THIS?" Almont looks in Rino's eyes and says, "He's right, this isn't helping us find her at all." Rino extends his hand and Almont takes his hand and they shake hands in a non-verbal agreement to stop their stupidity. Simon says, "I'm happy to see that you've agreed to stop the stupidity of this situation. Now, we need to focus. Come inside." Simon opens the front door to the Paper Book Library and they all walk inside.

Once in the library, the dream librarian smiles at Rino in a friendly way and looks at Simon and Almont in a disagreeing way. The dream librarian says, "Almont Alldream and Simon Dreamlee, I hope you two aren't up to any forbidden book researches." Simon says, "No, I didn't know that last book was forbidden." They walk towards a library table and Rino whispers, "Forbidden books in Dreamville?" Simon whispers, "Yes, there's a whole section." Almont whispers, "Adults keep secrets from us." Simon says, "I'll say, Rino tell him what you found out this last night." The Dream Librarian says, "Shush... Boys you're in a library." They all hush for a few moments when Simon pulls out some old fashioned paper and pencils and writes. Look for the ancient texts written by Master MagicDream. He passes the note to Almont who then passes the note to Rino. They all look at each other and get up from the table to search through the multiple book shelves under A's and M's. Simon fingers through the M's when he sees he's just a few footsteps from the restricted, forbidden area of books. The hovering surveillance camera hovers by him and films him looking through the M's. Satisfied, the hovering surveillance camera hovers away from Simon. Simon finds nothing under M's and Almont comes up to him and whispers, "Nothing under A's." Rino comes up to them and whispers, "Nothing, I found nothing remotely about this Master MagicDream." Simon hushes them, "Shush." The hovering surveillance camera films the three of them for quite a long time, about fifteen minutes. They look through the M's again while they're being watched. Finally, the hovering surveillance device hovers away. They all breathe a sigh of relief. Almont walks out into the view of the dream librarian and observes her put up a plain paper sign with fancy hand writing that says she's gone for an hour for lunch. He watches her leave her desk. Almont whispers, "Hey, the dream librarians gone for lunch." Simon comes out and sees she's gone from her post. Rino comes out too and whispers, "You know what this means?" Simon says, "Yeah, all we have to do is trick the surveillance camera." Almont places his hand on a table with a black table cloth and gets an idea. Almont lifts the table cloth and looks at Simon. Simon says, "Great idea. Cover it when it hovers by and we'll have free reign to go through the forbidden books." Rino says, "Here it comes." Simon and Rino just make a bunch of incomprehensible sounds, "Blah, blue, blue, blah, blah, blah..." Simon and Rino create a perfect distraction that keeps the hovering surveillance camera's focus on them while Almont, who's behind the hovering security camera, steps on a chair and drapes the black table cloth over the hovering surveillance device. The surveillance camera just remains in a motionless, still hover as they walk into the forbidden books area to look through the M's and A's. Rino says, "Here, over here. I found something." Simon and Almont run up to Rino who holds up a book titled; Master MagicDream's Gargoyles. Simon says, "That's it. It has to be it." Almont says, "Read a few lines to be sure it's the one from your latest dream to come true." Rino says, "What? You dreamt about this book?" Simon says, "Look there's no time to explain, the dream librarian will be back any minute." Rino opens the book and reads out loud, "Lions are the most common non-native animal. I crafted two gargoyles, female and male, to look like a lion with the body of a human. In these times, the lion is linked to the sun, due to its golden mane bearing a striking similarity to the solar wreath of the sun. These two gargoyles shall be strength and endurance." Simon exclaims that's it quick hide it under your shirt." They all step out of the library and Simon and Rino go out of the library with the forbidden book. They wait on the front steps for Almont who stayed behind. They see the dream librarian park her hover car, get out and walk up the steps past them. She enters the front doors. Meanwhile, Almont who stayed behind, un-covers the hovering surveillance camera and puts the cloth on the table quickly before the hovering device could film him. Smiling, he walks out of the library past the dream librarian as she returns from her lunch hour and walks behind her desk. Almont exits the Paper Book Library.

Once they're all outside in front of the building, Almont says, "We better get out of here now." They all say, "Hover." Their hovers boards all start to hover and they get on their boards." Simon says, "Come to my house and we'll finish reading in my attic." They all say, "Hover forward. Hover fast." Rino says, "Hover left." Simon says, "Slow hover, Hover left." Almont says, "Slow hover, Hover left." Almont and Simon says, "Hover fast." All three hover quickly, past all the houses, including Almont's house right up to Simon's house. Simon says, "Slow hover. Hover left." Almont says, "Slow hover. Hover left." They both say, "Cease hover." Both their boards hover downward and they get off of their hover boards. Rino's waiting for them in front of the Dreamlee's front door. Simon says, "Okay we should go inside." They follow Simon up to his attic. Rino pulls out the book and places it on the small table. Simon opens the book and speed reads to himself past the words he heard in his dream. Almont asks,

"Do you know what you're looking for?" Simon hushes him, "Shush..." Simon reads on in silence when he finds what he considers proof. He starts to read out loud, "I, master MagicDream will name my gentle protectors. The male lion shall be named, Gargantua, the female lion shall be named, Lionessa the male wolf shall be named, Wartua, the female wolf shall be named Wolverina..." Simon stops and smiles. Almont asks, "What? What is it?" Simon says, "The females, those names were the names used by the two female voices I heard in my dream last night. It was the two female gargoyles." Almont says, "Okay then. Read on and out loud for us." Simon nods his head and reads on, "The male dog shall be named, Dartua, the female dog shall be named Dogerina, The male snake shall be named, Sartua, the female snake shall be named, Snakerina, the male goat shall be named, Larantua, the female goat shall be named, Goaterina, the male monkey shall be named, Martua, and the female monkey shall be named Monkerina." Rino interrupts and says, "Wait, those statues of Gargoyles have actual names?" Almont says, "This is what Simon's latest dream's telling him." Simon looks at them and continues reading out loud, "From this day forth they will live freely at night protecting the Outsiders and being Dreamville's direct contacts to the Outside world without fear of being murdered without proper reason." Rino says, "Come on, as if they live at night." Almont says, "I know, hard to believe even for me but maybe this book can present us with some proof." Simon keeps reading, "They shall travel the underground passages under Dreamville, follow them under Dream Mountain and straight out into the streets of the Outsiders now primitive villages. I, Master MagicDream, know that one day these Outsiders will have major cities they will call bustling metropolitans." Almont says, "That makes sense, that's what we saw in the looking window." Rino nods his head in agreement. Simon reads on, "My dream is to better our ability to communicate with the use of the gargoyles who can observe the Outsiders and come and tell us their needs. I'm so confidant of this vision of mine that I freely have decided to move into a home in the Outsiders world and walk among them as if I were one of them. This will be my last entry into a Dreamville book. My presence and my descendants will know of Dreamville but they too shall live with me in the Outside world that I now consider from this moment going forth as safe. I will bring my secret gems with me that permit the creatures to live freely during the daylight hours but they cannot ever be seen walking around during the day in the Outsiders world or they'll misinterpret these deliciously incredible creatures' intentions as horrifically evil." Simon goes silent as Almont and Rino wait for him to say something, anything really to break the silence. Simon says, "That's it. Almont do you remember when we saw all those jewels?" Almont says, "Yes I do." Simon says, "There were gems, way more than just fourteen of them but they were gems none the less." Rino asks, "Where?" Almont says, "In the secret passage ways under DreamRoyal Castle." Simon says, "We need to get those gems and bring the creatures to life during the day so they can explain why they took Jilla." Rino says, "Hey, hey, hey… You guys seriously think that these statues come to life and kidnapped Jilla?" Simon replies, "I have to believe my theory and believe they won't harm her too until I figure out what they want." Rino says, "I guess so seeing how we can't trust the new female dream squad chief." Almont says, "And why not?" Simon says, "Go ahead tell him." Rino says, "I found out by overhearing my father talking last night that the new dream squad chief is, in fact, Miss DreamNot and the ex dream squad chief's biological daughter." Almont says, "Whatever, she's his sister. Baby sister, isn't she?" Rino shakes his head in disagreement and Simon says, "I believe him, after all, look at the major secret the adults kept from us that we uncovered over a year ago." Almont says, "That you uncovered. I only followed everything that you needed me to do." Rino says, "This dream of yours, maybe, we should all view it and see what we as a group can come up with as answers." Simon adds, "Or clues. That's a good idea." They all run downstairs to the first floor and into the virtual viewing room. Unfortunately, there plan's disturbed by Simon's parents hover car hovering into the hover garage. The hovering clock hovers by indicating the time to be exactly four in the beginning of Sunday evening. Rino says, "I guess we're not viewing your dream then." Simon says, "My parents, no doubt, know about the whole fiasco between Miss DreamNot and the ex dream squad chief and, no doubt, know that the new female dream squad chief is their daughter so wait until they come inside. I'll invite them to view my dream too. I want to see their reaction."

Cheerfully, Mr. and Mrs. Dreamlee walk into their house and kiss. Simon covers his eyes as he usually does while Almont diverts his eyes elsewhere landing on pictures of Simon when he was a toddler. Almont pokes Rino and points at the picture. They have a giggle. Mr. Dreamlee says, "Oh dear, look we have an audience." Simon uncovers his eyes and says, "Very funny. However, I'd like you to be my audience for my latest dream to become true." Mr. and Mrs. Dreamlee smile and Simon, Almont and Rino walk towards the virtual viewing room. Almont whispers, "About to become truer than anyone really wants." Rino pokes Almont's stomach with his elbow. Simon, Almont and Rino go into the virtual viewing room. Simon places his computer chip sized, hand held computer into the pod to wake up Viadream. Viadream materializes on the virtual screen and says, "Hello Dreamlee family and friends. What may I do for you today?" Simon says, "Viadream please play my latest dream." Viadream squeals with delight and says, "Oh with absolute pleasure, enjoy your father's tweaks to my system and the three dimensional virtual adventure that is your dream Simon." Mr. Dreamlee says, "I made a few modifications and decided to test them out on you, my family, first but with Almont and Rino here I can get some great additional feedback, especially from you Rino DreamScifi." Viadream asks, "Ready?" Everyone says, "Ready Viadream." She starts to play Simon's dream as she sits in the corner to view the dream herself. Simon's dream begins and in the true three dimensional formats they all feel as if they are in the musical play as one of the characters. The ancient royals and the royal servants have their conversation and read the ancient text of Master MagicDream, the looking window appears and the scene of horror being inflicted on the gargoyles. The cruel song sung by the un-understanding Outsiders. The stage, the dancers, the scenes, the closing of the rock and as the face of the kidnapped girl flashes, with the lion faced gargoyle standing over her, the second song plays with the lyrics being sung by the same little boy of hope from Simon's dream of over a year ago. His dream fades and the room is filled with silence. The deafening silence breaks when Simon asks, "So dad, what do you think of my dream?" Mr. Dreamlee says, "It's quite dramatic. Quite good, eerily interesting but ah… I'm sure like the last dream like this you'll dream up the happy ending." Simon says, "Of course, I will." He looks at his mother and she says, "Simon, it's going to be a block buster I'm sure. You're so gifted my son." Simon says, "Is that all you have to say. Well… thank you so much. I appreciate your approval." Viadream says, "Will that be all Simon for today." Simon turns to the miniature girl and says, "Viadream, yes, of course, thank you so much too." Viadream yawns and says, "Very well, good night." She shuts off as Simon takes out his computer chip sized, hand held computer and he places it in his pocket. Mr. and Mrs. Dreamlee stand up and Mrs. Dreamlee says, "I better get dinner ready, if you boys will excuse me." Rino and Almont stumble over each other's words and try to say, "Ah sure…. No problem… Mrs. Mrs. Dreamlee." She leaves the virtual viewing room and Mr. Dreamlee asks, "So boys, be honest now. What did you think of the three dimensional concept?" Rino replies, "I liked it a lot. I thought it was three dimensionallicious." Almont says, "Yeah dreamalicious." Simon's dad looks at him and asks, "Son, what did you think?" Simon replies, "I think it's marketable and another Charles Dreamlee success story in the works." Mr. Dreamlee smiles and says, "Thanks boys, you guys are great." He walks out of the virtual viewing room into the kitchen. Simon looks at Rino and Almont and says, "Well what did you guys think of my dream?" Rino says, "The girl's face flashed for such a short second but I swear it was Jilla's face." Almont says, "I thought so too." They're all silent for a few moments and then Simon says, "I'm right about the gems. It's in the lyrics of the second song." Almont and Rino nod their heads in agreement. Almont says, "That same song says that they'll take two more. What do you think the little boy means by that?" Simon replies, "I don't know yet but I'll try and figure it out." Rino says" I think the better question is; who are the next two people that will be kidnapped by the perpetrators?" Simon says, "You really don't think that it's the gargoyles." Rino says, "I'm a scientific guy who needs more proof than some ancient text that for all we know could really just be this Master MagicDream's written compilation of a fictional story. Besides, with no absolute concrete proof that this guy ever really existed, Simon, you have nothing but a really cool, fictional, but cool story." Simon sighs and says, "So we have nothing but speculation according to you." Rino says, "Probably fictional speculation." Simon says, "Well, the lyrics in my dream say that Jilla will not be harmed. I say that if two more Dreamvillians get kidnapped on Monday like in the lyrics indicate that we need to dig for indisputable evidence that these creatures come alive before ruling this theory out all together." They nod their heads in agreement. Simon says, "Rino come up to my attic one more time, I want to show you my notations regarding the gargoyle statues." They all go upstairs and Simon hands Rino his observations. Rino looks them over and comments, "Wow, you know if you weren't a musically inclined dreamer you'd fair well as a scientist." Simon says, "Thanks, that's great but what about my observations." Rino says, "Well let me know if there's any change from your observations of the statues from these last entries when you observe them tomorrow morning." Simon says, "That's all you have to say." Rino says, "For now, yeah." Simon says, "I know what I have to do. I have to film them waking up and come alive. I'll stay up all night if I have too." Almont says, "I wish I could do that with you but I can't, in fact, I promised my mother I'd be home an hour ago." Rino says, "Yeah I got to get home too." Simon walks them downstairs to the first floor and out the front door. Rino gets on his hover board and says, "Hover, Still hover." Almont says, "Hover to me." He gets on his board and says, "Still hover." Rino says, "Look Simon, have sweet dreams." Almont says, "Yeah, sweet dreams Simon." Simon says, "I can count on you guys if I find concrete indisputable proof right?" They both say, "Absolutely." Rino says, "Hover right. Hover fast." He's gone. Almont says, "Simon…" Simon says, "Don't worry Almont, we'll find her." Almont looks at him with a defeated look and says, "Hover left. Hover forward." Almont's gone for the night too. Mrs. Dreamlee comes outside and says, "Now that your friends are gone dear, you should come in for your supper." Simon turns around and goes inside his home. He closes the front door behind him, locks it and walks into the kitchen. He sits at the kitchen table and plays with his food. Mr. Dreamlee says, "Aren't you hungry Simon?" Simon replies, "Actually, no, I'm not hungry at all, really." Mrs. Dreamlee says, "At least drink your milk." Simon takes his glass of milk and chugs it down. Mr. Dreamlee puts the hovering virtualcast on and the media clown beams from the hovering virtual newscaster. The media clown says, "Although everything's calm, pristine, and dreamily dreamy in Dreamville there's still no sign of the missing MusiDream girl, Jilla. The dream squad chief still has no comment but assures everyone that this heinous crime has not been perpetrated by Dreamville's banished enemies Miss DreamNot and or the ex dream squad chief. Please everyone have sweet dreams this dreamy Sunday night." The virtualcast shuts off and hovers into its rechargeable station. The hovering clock hovers by indicating the time to be eight thirty-eight Sunday night. Simon looks at the clock and says, "Well, I'm going to go upstairs for the evening until you say to go to bed." He walks upstairs into the attic and observes the still frozen statues of the gargoyles through his hovering telescope. Simon notices that he hears nothing at all, not even the quiet humming sound of the dream squad cops combing the streets of Dreamville in search of Jilla. Simon whispers, "They've given up." He hears his mother's footsteps and he starts going down the stairs and meets her at the halfway point of the staircase. He says, "I know time for bed. She kisses him on his forehead and they walk down to the second level. Simon enters his bedroom and says, "Sweet dreams mom." She replies, "Sweet dreams Simon." She closes his door and he turns off his lights but does not attach the dream catcher to his head and he places a sheet of paper between his head and his pillow as he lies down on his bed. He pets Boomboom Booya who's like a permanent fixture in his room, particularly, on his bed. He quietly waits for his parents to go to bed too. Simon whispers, "I'll shut my eyes but only for a moment." He hears his parents go into their bedroom and shut their door. He wastes an additional ten minutes before getting up, he gets up, opens his bedroom door and through the darkness, he tiptoes up to the attic. He looks through his hovering telescope and observes the gargoyle statues non-stop until midnight. At midnight he turns on his virtual film recorder with night time lights and places it by him on the window sill. He looks through his telescope again and sees the statues are gone from their spots. He writes, five minutes past twelve, every single one of them is missing. Then he hears wisps of large wings in the air and points his telescope upwards, he sees the living breathing gargoyles flying through the dreamily clear, star filled Dreamvillian night sky. He grabs his virtual film recorder and begins to focus in on the beautiful spectacle that is indisputable proof that they come alive. He silently counts them, and whispers, "Eleven. There should thirteen with the exclusion of the stolen gargoyle, Gargantua." Suddenly, he hears an unexpected deep voice say, "No, now there are ten of us." Simon keeps the virtual film recorder aimed forward as he lowers his head and before him, the flying, breathing, speaking, and living male monkey gargoyle smiles at him with crisp white teeth. Simon's stunned and speechless but manages to mutter, "Martua." Martua says, "Yes, that's right. I can't let you tell people we come alive, at least, not yet anyway." Martua blows the same golden dust into Simon's face that Gargantua had done over a year ago. Simon releases his grip on the virtual film recorder that hovers into a dark black corner making it difficult for Martua to see where it went. Wartua flies up to Martua and says, "Come on, we have to go." Simon's still barely conscience says, "Go where? Where have you taken Jilla?" Martua and Wartua have already flown away from Simon's window and didn't hear his questions. Simon inhales the golden dust that still floats around him like glitter and falls to sleep. Boomboom Booya climbs the stairs to the attic, licks Simon's face, barks at the hovering virtual film recorder, "woof" and lies down beside him and goes to sleep too.

Chapter Five – Simon's Plan

Monday morning, Simon's awoken by his distraught mother who says, "Simon Dreamlee what are you doing sleeping on the attic floor?" She taps her foot in disapproval. Simon watches her foot tap as he gets up into a sitting position. Boomboom Booya gets up and licks Simon's face. He says, "I'm not sure why I'm up here." His mother says, "Young teen aged boy, it's time to get you ready for school. Quickly now or you'll be late." Simon gets up off the attic floor and sees the still hovering virtual film maker in the corner of the roof of the attic. He grabs it and brings it into his room. He pushes save and shuts it off as he puts it into its protective carrying bag. He slings the strap over his shoulder, puts his computer sized, hand held computer into his pocket along with his virtual communicator. He looks around his room and then walks out, walks downstairs to the first floor and into the kitchen where his parents are finishing their breakfast. Mrs. Dreamlee says, "Simon, don't just stand there, come and eat your carrot cake muffin." Simon grabs it and says, "I'll eat it on my way to Dreamtrue School, happy Monday!" He quickly goes out the back door and shuts the door before his parents could say anything more about his overnighter on the attic floor. He says, "Hover to me." His hover board hovers from the front of the house to the backyard where Simon eats his breakfast quickly. He steps on his hover board as he swallows his last morsel of carrot cake muffin and says, "Hover forward. Hover slowly. Hover left. Hover forward. Hover slowly. Hover right. Hover forward. Hover fast." He hovers quickly down his street to his and Simon's crossroads. Simon says, "Hover slowly. Still hover." He waits for Almont to arrive on his hover board. Simon begins realizing that Almont's really late. Simon says, "Oh un-dreamy dreams, Almont's one of the two." Just as he finishes his thought out loud he hears Almont yell, "Happy Monday Simon." Simon sighs and watches as he hovers up to him. Almont says, "Still hover." He forgets to commands his hover board to slow down and goes flying over Simon into Mrs.

LandDream's prized, dreamy pink rose bushes." Almont yells, "Ah... thorns." Simon says, "Almont your hover boards gone rogue." Almont yells, "Cease hover." His board hovers to the ground two houses from the crossroads. Simon's in a still hover right beside Almont so he extends his hand to Almont and helps him up. Simon says, "Happy Monday." Almont rolls his eyes and says, "Oh un-dreamy dreams." He looks at his hover board and says, "Hover to me." He gets on his hover board and says, "Still hover." Almont asks, "So did you get proof?" Simon says, "Proof of what?" Almont says, "Oh how dreamily unfunny of you. Proof of the living, breathing gargoyles, of course, well did you?" Simon replies, "I don't remember. In fact, I don't remember much about last night and I woke up on the attic floor this morning." Almont says, "Well then why do you have your virtual film recorder?" Simon says, "We should get to school and on our first break, we'll see what I filmed last night." They both say, "Hover forward. Fast hover." They quickly hover down the street to DreamHappy Street, they both say, "Hover slow. Hover left. Hover forward." They hover into the hover parkade and say, "Cease Hover." Their hover boards hover downwards into the solar panel grids to recharge. They step off of their hover boards and start to walk on the sidewalk towards the front doors of their beloved school. As Simon's about to open the doors, the doors fling open by a stampeding group of dream inclined students who all seem to be rushing for their hover bikes, hover boards and on foot for their homes. Almont yells, "What's going on?" None of them seem to hear them with all the commotion and noise they're making. Simon says, "What else in Dreamville happened that we're obviously clueless about?" They see Rino come out of the school. He's being pushed and shoved as the other students continuously keep rushing out of Dreamtrue School. Simon says, "There's Rino. He'll know what's going on." Rino spots them and walks towards them as quickly as he can. Rino says, "Almont, Simon, have you heard?" Simon says, "No, we're confused right now." Almont asks, "Yeah, heard what?" Rino replies, "Two more Dreamvillians have been kidnapped." Rino stops talking and looks at them both. Almont says, "Well come on, tell us who." Simon says, "They don't know who yet, do they?" Rino says, "King DreamRoyal had everyone gather in the dream coliseum to announce the un-dreamy news that school's cancelled until the three kidnapped victims are found and safely returned to their homes. He said that it would be best if we were all safe in our homes and to lock our doors, windows and other points of entry into our homes until our parents come home from their dreamy careers." Simon asks, "And, he never said who the two other kidnapped victims are?" Rino nods his head and says, "Yes, that's right. I think this hasn't even been leaked to the media clowns yet either which is why there hasn't been any virtualcast informing us of the current situation." Almont says, "Simon has a virtual film to show us from last night." Simon says, "Ah yeah… I don't know what though." Rino says, "What do you mean, you don't know what?" Simon says, "Exactly, that. I don't remember what I did and why I woke up on my attic floor this morning." Rino and Almont look at each other and shrug their shoulders. Simon un-zips his carrying bad and pulls out the virtual film recorder. They're alone standing in front of the school and everything's gone silent. Almont says, "Eerie." Simon sets up his hovering virtual recorder to hover stilly in the air at eye level and it projects what he saw Sunday night. Rino and Almont watch with jaws dropped as they see with their own eyes the ten flying gargoyles in the Dreamville night sky but they're even more astonished by Martua once he starts talking and Wartua he also starts talking. Almont says, "What's that gold dust that Martua blew on you?" Simon who vaguely remembers the night but now that he sees it on film comes to a revelation and says, "That dust is some kind of memory eraser that puts Dreamvillians to sleep. That's why I had no recollection of this ever happening when I woke up this morning." Rino says, "Oh my dreams so it is true. The kidnapping culprits may very well be these creatures, these gargoyles described as gentle." Almont asks, "If they're supposedly so gentle, why are they kidnapping innocent Dreamvillians?" Simon replies, "They're looking for attention from someone, someone they think can help them." Rino says, "Why not just reveal themselves to that person instead?" Simon replies, "I think they feel they need leverage to keep themselves out of harm's way." Almont asks, "I wonder who they want to help them?" Rino with his scientific mind says, "Okay well Simon's established that they do in fact come to life but we don't have any evidence that they've kidnapped anybody. We need concrete proof." Almont asks, "How, in all dreams, are we going to do that?" Almont's virtualcast goes off and beams the image of the media clown at King DreamRoyal's house. The media clown asks, "King DreamRoyal do you have any idea who would steal yet another two of your gargoyles?" King DreamRoyal replies, "I don't know at all who would want to steal my precious statues. More importantly, I don't know why they would kidnap Miss LossDream either. I'm hoping and counting on the new dream squad chief and her dream squad cops to come up with the answer but so far to no avail." The media clown says, "Why would anyone want to kidnap and hopefully not harm

Jilla MusiDream, Miss LossDream and Dee FictiveDream? It's not so dreamy in Dreamville today this sunny Monday. Will Dreamville ever have another dreamy royal wedding celebration or is this the end of the royal bloodline or worse the beginning of the end of Dreamville?" Almont turns off his virtualcast and Rino exclaims, "Dee's been kidnapped too. Oh my un-dreamy dreams, nightmares. Why kidnap her?" Almont replies, "I can't think of a reason why Dee would be kidnapped." They stand in silence for a few minutes until Simon says, "I have an idea but it includes our need for some of my father's unpatented technology." Almont says, "Fine, I'll risk it." Rino says, "Yeah, whatever health risk there might be is worth the risk to find the girls." Simon says, "Hover to me." His hover board hovers to him and he steps on his board. He then says, "Follow me to my house. Hover forward." Rino and Almont voice command their boards all the way to Simon's front door.

At Simon's house, they all command their hover boards to "cease hover" and go inside the Dreamlee's house through the front door. Once inside, they follow Simon to the basement instead of the attic. Once in the basement, they wait for him to tell them about his plan. Simon turns around to face them and says, "Okay, guys, I trust both of you to not tell anyone about this place." He opens the first door in the basement and they enter into a science lab with multiple robotic prototypes. Rino exclaims, "Wow, I'm in Mr. Dreamlee's secret science lab aren't I?" Simon looks at him and says, "This is hush, hush, understand." Rino checks out all the high tech gadgets and he says, "I couldn't have dreamed about these scientific wondrous advancements myself if I commanded myself to dream them to come true. I'm wonderstruck. Your dad's so cool Simon." Almont says, "Absolutely, my dreams, all of these gadgets are… What are some of these things?" Rino opens his mouth to begin to explain but Simon intervenes and says, "Ah Rino we don't have time for scientific explanations." Rino nods his head in agreement. He says, "Cool by me." Almont says, "Alright then, Simon, why have you brought us here?" Simon pulls open the far right stainless steel drawer from a long narrow counter and takes out three pairs of goggles. Rino says, "Goggles?" Almont says, "What's so special about those?" Simon says, "My father had a dream to develop night time vision for the regular Dreamvillian eye. He went based on the concept of an eagle's eyesight." Rino exclaims, "They function?" Simon says, "I'm counting on it." Almont says, "Okay so what's your plan?" Simon says, "We need them to kidnap another Dreamvillian so we can follow them to the location of Jilla, Miss LossDream and Dee." Almont asks, "Who are we going to get them to kidnap if they've kidnapped everyone they want? That is, if your dream's accurate?" Simon looks at Rino and then at Almont and he says, "They'll kidnap a decoy." Rino asks, "Who do you have in mind." Simon looks at Almont and Almont reacts, "Ah no, no, no, no, I'm not putting myself out there in the middle of the night to be carried away by some foreign, strange, creatures that until now were nothing but fictional characters carved into rock statues." Simon says, "Almont we'll be right behind you following with the night vision goggles and these devices." Rino says, "What are those?" Simon says, "You have to swear that you never ever speak to anyone about these devices." He holds his hand out, Rino puts his hand on top of his, Almont looks at the both of them and puts his hand on top of Rino's and they all say, "We solemnly, dreamily swear never ever to talk about these devices." Simon says, "Okay, these two devices will camouflage Rino and my voice so we can talk while following you and the Gargoyles will not hear us." Almont says, "Great. That's great. But what if they see you and capture you too?" Simon replies, "Good question and that's what these two devices here are going to help us do." Rino says, "They don't. Do they?" Almont asks, "Do what? What do those devices do?" Simon says, "Don't lose patience boys. These two devices will make Rino and me invisible." Rino says, "What?" Simon says, "Watch." He squeezes the simple, small oval device that fits in the palm of his hand and disappears right before their eyes. Rino and Almont gasp and Simon un-squeezes the device. Rino says, "Your father's a genius." Simon says, "Now remember, I have no idea what the possible side effects are so you'd be coming with me on this journey at your own risk Rino." Rino says, "Like I said before I want to help find not only Jilla but Dee and Miss LossDream too." Almont says, "His risk you're worried about, what about my risk factor? I'm the one about to be snagged by the Gargoyles." Simon pats his best friend on the shoulder and says, "And we think you're brave for volunteering." Simon winks at Rino who smiles. Almont says, "Brave. Yeah it is brave of me isn't it? Jilla will really think that too. Won't she?" Rino puts his hand on Almont's opposite shoulder and says, "She definitely will think of you as her hero, Almont." Almont stands there smiling as he explains the picture in his head, "Jilla's face will light up when I arrive with the kidnapping Gargoyle and once I explain everything about how I've come to rescue her from death she'll be so happy with me." Rino says, "Be prepared for smooching." Almont says, "Smooching? Gross, she's a girl." Simon and Rino look at each other and laugh, "Ha-ha. Ha-ha." Almont asks, "What's so funny?" Simon says, "Nothing Almont. Okay, we have to get out of here before my father catches us in here." He closes the open drawer and motions them towards the door. Once they're all in the main part of the basement, Simon closes the door." Rino says, "I'm surprised that your father doesn't lock this door." Simon says, "He does. Try and open the door." Rino touches the door knob and attempts to turn the knob. He gets shocked." Almont and Simon laugh as Rino recovers from the small jolt. "Ha-ha. Ha-ha." Rino says, "You could've just told me instead of making me the demonstrator." Simon replies, "Your scientific mind would've wanted to test it out anyway." Rino smiles and says, "You're right Simon. You're absolutely right." They all go upstairs to the main floor. Simon says, "We should go wait in the thick gooseberry bushes just outside of the gates into King DreamRoyal's yard until nightfall." They walk outside and step on their hover boards.

Simon says, "Hover still." Almont says, "Hover still." Rino says, "Hover still." Almont says, "Well general we're awaiting your command." Simon and Rino look at him and Almont says, "What? Come on, I'm about to be carried away by the Gargoyles to who knows where, where they'll do who knows what to me, I'm aloud a sense of humor." Simon says, "Hover left. Hover forward." Rino says, "Hover left. Hover forward." Almont says, "Okay here it goes. Hover left. Hover forward." They hover towards DreamRoyal hill. Simon reaches the bottom of the hill and says, "Still hover." Rino arrives first and says, "Still hover." Almont arrives last and also says, "Still hover." Almont continues to say, "What's the hold up?" Simon looks up DreamRoyal hill and says, "King DreamRoyal's leaving his castle." They watch his hover car coming down the hill, he stops, hovers in front of them, rolls down his window and asks, "What are you boys doing outside away from the safety of your homes?" Simon says, "We'll be okay King DreamRoyal." Rino says, "Yeah, we're three together." Almont says, "If anyone tries to kidnap us will overpower them." King DreamRoyal says, "Go home boys. I mean it. Even, if Rino's babysitting you." He hovers away. They wait until he's no longer in view. Almont says, "Do I look like I need a babysitter?" Simon says, "Never mind that." Almont says, "I can't, our king just insulted us, well, me for certain." Rino laughs, "Ha-ha. Ha-ha." Simon says, "Hover up." Rino says, "Hover up." Almont gulps and says, "Hover up." They hover up the hill until they reach the gooseberry bushes. Simon says, "Cease hover." Rino says, "Cease hover." Almont says, "Cease hover." They all step off of their hover boards. Simon puts his hover board in the bush and so do Rino and Almont. Simon crawls into the bush and so do Rino and Almont. They wait in silence. The silence is broken when Almont says, "Hey there's two eagles." Simon says, "Yeah so?" Almont says, "Well if one of them takes me I'd like to know their names." Simon says, "I didn't read their names out loud." Almont asks, "Did you read their names at all." Simon says, "The male eagle's named, Eagantua and the female eagle's named, Eaglerina." Almont complains, "We should've eaten before coming here." Rino pulls chocolate bars out of his pocket and hands one to Almont and to Simon. Simon says, "Thanks." Almont says, "Thanks." Rino says, "Since the famous event of over a year ago, I always stock up on chocolate bars every morning. I have four more in my pocket." Almont says, "Yum... Oh my dreams, I was hungry." Simon's still chewing on the first piece he put in his mouth. He puts the rest in his pocket. Rino says, "Here Almont. Have another chocolate bar to put in your pocket. No doubt Jilla and the others will be hungry." Almont takes the chocolate bar and puts it in his pocket. Rino says, "Actually, take two." Almont says, "Thank you." Simon looks at his watch and says, "We're going to be here awhile before nightfall, it's only three in the afternoon." Rino says, "If they wake up at nightfall then we only have about six to seven hours to wait." Simon says, "Yeah but they only wake up at midnight. At least, that's when they woke up last night." Almont lies down and says, "Then I suggest we get our sleep now." Rino lies down and says, "That's a good idea." Simon lies down as well and they take a nap. While they all nap, Simon begins to dream, hearing the two songs over and over in his head as they fade and a new one begins with yet another angelic voice singing the beautiful lyrics.

Little truth dreamer, that's you
Please don't be scared
We need your help
Come to the Outside world through ancient passage
And meet us,
Friends of the Gargoyles
Future friends of yours
We wish to live amongst
Dreamvillians freely
And dreamily too

Little truth dreamer, that's you
Please don't be frightened
We need your help

Come to the Outside world through ancient passage
And greet us
Chimeras
Master MagicDream's last dream, come true
We live as captives
We wish to be free
We wish to dream too

Little truth dreamer, that's you
Please don't hesitate
We need your help
Come to the Outside world through ancient passage
And defeat us
Kidnappers
Cursed by a cruel joke
We're that family's prisoners
We wish to be your servants
We wish to defeat out common enemies too

Truth dreamer, that's you
Please come
Please come
Quickly,
Swiftly,
Safely,
Come.

Monday night, Simon's awoken by Rino who's shaking him and just as Simon's about to say something, Rino covers his mouth. Once Simon calms down he removes his hand. Simon looks at Almont who's still asleep too. Simon whispers, "How do we wake him up?" Rino does the same thing to Almont who takes a little longer to calm down but once he does, Rino takes his hand off of his mouth too. Almont whispers, "Nightmare of a way to wake a guy." Rino shrugs his shoulders and whispers, "That's all I could think of dude." Simon hushes them, "Shush… Midnight's approaching." Simon looks at Almont. Like a dummy, Almont looks back at him. Simon whispers, "Almont that's your cue." Almont says, "Ah yeah, right." Almont stands up and walks out of the bushes to wait in front of one of the Gargoyles. He talks to himself, "Alright there snakes,

I hate snakes, and I think I'd prefer to be kidnapped by one of you cute goats. After all, goats are harmless." Rino whispers, "What's he muttering about out there?" Simon whispers, "I don't know but it's time to shut up right about now." Sure enough, the shiny gargoyles begin to move around in the moonlight. Almont says, "Oh dreams, un-dreamy dreams, they're coming to life." Simon whispers, "Come on Almont be brave don't run." Almont stands in the middle of the awakening Gargoyles, he shakes but manages not to scream when the male snake puts his hand on his shoulder and says, "What or who do we have here?" Almont turns around but is muted with fear, unable to speak, he's swooped up by the Sartua as he flaps his wings and becomes air born. The other gargoyles look at Almont and the female lion, Lionessa says, "He's not part of the plan. They don't want him." The male wolf, Wartua says, "We have no choice but to bring him. He's witnessed us come to life and we don't know where he lives to safely bring him to his bed once we blow the golden dust on him." Sartua says, "Quickly now, we have to fly there and be back in three hours." They all lift off into the air and start flying up into the sky. Simon and Rino look at each other and rapidly put on their night vision goggles. Simon says, "Manual Hover." Rino says, "Manual Hover." Suddenly, the male monkey, Martua, says to the female goat, Goaterina, "Hey, did you hear that? It sounded like it came from the bushes." Simon looks at Rino and signals to turn on the voice camouflage device and the cloaking device. Just as Martua and Goaterina fly in front of the bushes, the devices begin to fully function. Martua reacts, "Huh… must've been my imagination playing tricks on me." He flies away to join the rest of the group. Goaterina lingers but eventually flies away to join the rest of the group stretching their wings in the Dreamville night sky. Almont gains courage and Simon and Rino hear him ask, "So where are you going to take me?" Sartua laughs and says, "Ha-ha. Listen to this one. He's asking where we're taking him." The male wolf, Wartua says, "So tell him. I see no harm in telling him." Sartua looks down at Almont and says, "To the Outsiders world to be with your fellow Dreamvillian captives." Almont screams, "The Outside world, you can't bring me there; that will mean I'm banished from Dreamville forever if you bring me there." Wartua says, "Then you'll know now how our friends feel." Sartua says, "Okay, get going everyone." They start flying northward. Simon steps on his hover board and so does Rino. Simon says, "Follow those Gargoyles." Rino says, "Can do." They hover out of the gooseberry bushes and follow behind the gargoyles by keeping track of them with the night time vision goggles.

Simon says, "With our success of our ploy to deceive the gargoyles into kidnapping Almont and tricking them into leading us to Jilla, Miss LossDream and Dee, we should be home by tomorrow." Rino says, "We can dream, hope." They, throughout the night, pursue the flying Gargoyle kidnappers and their friend Almont. The calmly circulating air wisps past them as they fly high in the air. Simon says, "Rino we have to catch up with them." Rino says, "I know but they fly so fast." Simon says, "It's a good thing we have these eagle eyed night time viewing goggles." Simon and Almont fly over the residential area of Dreamville. They pursue the gargoyles over the shopping centers of Dreamville, over the dream squad station, over the Hoverway and over the dream parliamentary building. Simon says, "Look there's the Dreamville Films and Movies Production Company on Dreamwood Boulevard." Rino says, "We're nearing the Dreamville fields." They follow intently as the Gargoyles fly smoothly and effortlessly through the air. They notice them slowing down. Simon says, "This is our chance to catch up." Rino says, "Agreed." They fly quickly forward, towards the Gargoyles until they're right on the very edge of their airborne conversation circle. Simon and Rino can hear their conversation. Sartua says, "We're nearing the edge of Dreamville and will soon be flying over the forbidden forest wall Dreamvillian." He looks down at Almont and he asks, "What's your name Dreamvillian boy?" Almont mutters, "Almont." Sartua says, "Almont. That's an interesting name. Does it symbolize anything?" Almont says, "I think my parents told me once that it means the dreamy strength of a mountain." Simon says, "Huh, interesting. I didn't know that." Rino says, "Me neither." Simon says, "I wonder what my name means." Rino says, "You don't know." Wartua says, "Did you hear that? Who said that?" Simon quickly says, "You're your voice camouflage device is turned off." Rino quickly turns it back on. Wartua flies in between the two of them practically knocking Simon off of his hover board. He struggles with his footing but gained his balance back and stabilizes himself. Wartua flies back through the two of them again but this time Simon's prepared. Wartua flies back to the circle and Simon says, "That was too close for comfort." Rino says, "Are you alright?" Simon replies, "I got shaken and thrown off balance but I gained my footing back." Rino says, "My name symbolizes little king." Simon says, "Wow that's pretty significant isn't it. You know I think I remember now what my name means; it means to be heard, or to hear." Rino says, "That's interesting too." Simon looks down and says, "Looks like we're right over the forbidden wall of the forest now." Rino says, "Ah Simon, where are the

Gargoyles" Simon looks around everywhere and says, "They're gone." Rino says, "No look they're just up ahead." Simon says, "Okay let's concentrate." Simon looks all around him and sees all kinds of golden dust in the air around them. Simon realizes what kind of dust it is and shouts to Rino, "Rino, quickly put your hover board in still hover mode and then hover down." Rino asks, "What for?" Simon getting drowsy says, "Just do it, trust me." Simon falls to sleep. With pure adrenaline pumping through his veins from the rush of the chase; Rino manages to mumble, "Simon, what's happening?" Rino does what Simon said to do just as he too starts falling to sleep. Simon can't answer Rino's drowsily proposed question because he's already fast asleep on his hover board. Their hover boards get just above the tree tops when Simon falls off and into some thick bushes. Rino drops his invisibility device into the bushes and then Rino falls off next, he falls on a large tree limb and then into the bushes next to Simon. They don't wake up. In the nearby distance, a large pack of ferocious forbidden forest wall wolves, are howling at the full moon. In mid-air over the bushes, a single eagle sits on Simon's hovering board, watching the ground below. In the bushes, Simon dreams. In his dream the line "Come to the Outside world through ancient passage" resounds loudly in his head as it repeats over and over again

Truth dreamer, that's you
Please come
Please come
Quickly,
Swiftly,
Safely,
Come.

Come to the Outside world through ancient passage.
Come to the Outside world through ancient passage.
Come to the Outside world through ancient passage.
Come to the Outside world through ancient passage.
Come to the Outside world through ancient passage.
Come to the Outside world through ancient passage.
Come to the Outside world through ancient passage.
Come to the Outside world through ancient passage.
Come to the Outside world through ancient passage.
Come to the Outside world through ancient passage.

Chapter Six – Escape From The Forbidden Forest Wall

In the bushes, still fast asleep, still dreaming, Simon's dream goes silent and then nothing, blackness but voices fill the blackness. There's only one discernible, familiar voice and that voice's Almont. A male voice says, "We've passed the forbidden forest wall and we'll soon be reaching our destination." The sounds of the winds pick up and the same male voice says, "Don't worry, you never really get used to the Outsiders fierce winds but in a way they're refreshing." Another male voice says, "Sartua, we spread the golden dust all around the forbidden forest wall like you said to do." Sartua says, "Good, Gargantua will soon learn not to worry about if we're doing our jobs when he's away. Good work Wartua." Almont asks, "What does the gold dust do?" Sartua says, "Well why not tell you, after all when we use it on you and your friends, you'll not remember me or any conversations we have." Almont says, "What do you mean?" Sartua replies, "Exactly that. The gold dust is an antiquities dust left to us by my Master MagicDream. He dreamed it up and created this non-exhaustible dust to aid us in protecting Dreamvillians and your borders, only, we used to protect from the Outside world and not from within Dreamville like we do now. The effects of the golden dust are harmless but effective." Almont asks, "What exactly does the golden dust do to Dreamvillians?" Sartua laughs and says, "Ha-ha. My you're an inquisitive one aren't you? The golden dust makes you forget ever coming in contact with us gargoyles by putting you in a transient deep restful sleep." Almont mutters, "Oh my dreams." Sartua asks, "What does that mean." Almont says, "Oh it's just an expression of despair, or delight, or anything depending in what context it's needed." Sartua says, "I see. Well your friends will sleep well little Almont and here we've arrived." Almont asks, "What's that building?" Sartua replies, "It's a church, one of many and even more denominations."

Almont asks, "Denom… Denomin…." Then the sound of the gargoyles giant wings, "whoosh" fills Simon's dream as they lift off and start to fly again. Almont asks, "Where have you brought me now?" A friendly, recognizable female voice that Simon has heard in his previous dreams says, "I'm Lionessa. I'll bring you to your friends Almont." Almont and Lionessa's footsteps fill Simon's dream. Almont comments, "These are large, tall and long corridors, multiple rooms. Am I in a mansion? These are the oddest objects, paintings, posters, and memorabilia I've ever seen in all my dream filled life." Lionessa says, "Our creator was a great magician as you can tell by his collectibles. Every one of these objects, were used at one time or another in magic shows." Almont exclaims, "Wow, he did well for himself outside of Dreamville." Lionessa says, "Indeed." The sounds of their footsteps stop and the sounds of taps on a wooden wall fill his dream. Lionessa hushes Almont, "Shush, this is a secret door." Their footstep start again as they enter the secret room, suddenly, there's only one set of footsteps. Almont says, "Must be daylight outside now." Sounding horrified at a discovery he's made, Almont exclaims to himself, "Oh my un-dreamy dreams, nightmares of the worse kind, Jilla you've been turned into a statue, Miss LossDream and Dee too. I feel oddly cold. I'm shivering, stiffening and hardening, oh my, worse nightmares of nightmares." Silence, blackness and humdrum fill the ending moments of Simon's dream.

Tuesday morning day breaks, the bushes where Simon and Rino sleep are surrounded by the vicious wolves, Simon begins to stir, rustling the bushes and drawing attention to his not yet fully conscience self. Wolves sniff and sniff the bushes where Simon lies to catch the scent of their next fresh kill, their next fresh meal. Simon yawns, stretches, opens his eyes to see the sniffing nostril of a large wolf right close to his face but he's still hidden in the bush. Startled, surprised and slightly displaced, he slowly looks around but he can't see Rino anywhere. Being as silent as he can be, he watches the wolves. If it hadn't been for his dream during the night, he'd of forgotten how he got where he currently is but remarkably he fully remembers. Despite this, panic builds inside of him but he remains calm even though the dire situation grows more and more dangerous as more and more of the wolves gather besides the one that has obviously caught Simon's deliciously tantalizing scent. Simon looks around for his hover board but two of the wolves are standing right on his board and it's still programmed to manual hover mode. He can't command it to come to him. Wolves are gathering closer and closer to the bush where he lies as still as he possibly can. Realizing that he can no longer remain in a still lying position he sits up as the pack of wolves prepare to pounce on the bush to attack him and eat him. Simon watches them get distracted by a loud sound of some forest creature rustling the bushes loudly on the other side of the small separation between the trees. They all run towards the sound. Simon decides that's a safe moment if ever there is one to get his hover board. He quickly switches it to voice recognition hover mode. As he stands up with his hover board in his hands, he's struck by a rock. Simon exclaims, "Owe." Rino sticks his face out of the bush that was besides Simon's bush and starts to laugh, "Ha-ha." Simon says, "Rino, thank dreams, you're okay." Rino says, "I should say the same about you. If I hadn't of thrown that rock way over there, you'd be wolf chow right now." Simon says, "Thanks Rino, I really owe you one." Rino says, "No you don't, I owed you from last year around this time." Simon says, "Maybe it's not a question about owing, it's just being a good friend." Rino hovers out of his bush and up to Simon and extends his hand out. Simon takes his hand and they shake hands. Rino says, "Now, do you mind explaining to me why I've woken up in the middle of the forbidden forest." Simon asks, "You don't remember what we did last night?" Rino says, "No, I don't remember anything." Simon says, "Not anything at all?" Rino says, "No, all I remember is looking at some video proving the gargoyles do come to life, your plan to hide in the bushes just outside of King DreamRoyal's yard and hiding in them." Simon says, "That's a fair good amount. Enough for me to tell you we chased the gargoyles because they did kidnap Almont like we planned and when we flew over the forbidden forest wall they spread golden dust in the air. We flew through the golden dust and ended up falling here and sleeping the rest of the night." Rino says, "If I hadn't of just woken up in the forbidden wall, I wouldn't believe this story myself." Simon says, "Never mind that, we've now gotten Almont kidnapped, on purpose, and we still have no idea where they've taken any of our friends." They hover stilly just above the ground in silence pondering what their next move should be when the pack of twelve wolves creep up on them and pounce. Rino yells, "Hover up. Simon, say hover up." Rino starts hovering upwards. Simon startled by the wolves coming at him yells, "Hover up." Seemingly like an eternity for his hover board to start hovering upwards, it finally does just as a wolf bites Simon's pant leg. The large, heavy, toothy wolf hovers upwards with Simon and his hover board. Simon loses his footing, about to fall over and downward into the pack of wolves to become their breakfast, lunch and supper, Rino says, "Fast hover." Rino hovers quickly towards the wolf and knocks him. The grey and black eyed wolf swings in the air, Simon's pant leg rips and the wolf falls to the ground landing on his back. The wolf gets up and licks his wounds, a gash from Rino's hover board. Simon can't get his footing, balance or stability stabilized and falls towards the wolf pack. Rino yells, "Hover backwards." He hovers backwards and grabs Simon's hand. They hold on to each other with every muscle in their bodies as Rino slowly goes downward to the point where the wolves are jumping and just about nipping at Simon's feet. Rino yells, "Hover upwards, Hover fast." He holds on as tightly as he can. Simon yells, "I'm losing my grip." Rino yells, "Hold on." Simon says, "I can't." Rino yells, "Yes you can." Rino hovers upwards and yells grab onto your hover board." Simon reaches out and grabs his hover board that's still going upwards. He says, "Still Hover." In the still hover, Simon manages to climb on and stand on his hover board. Rino yells from a distance, "Come on Simon. We need to get out of here. Look behind you." Simon turns around and sees a giant flock of Eagles to numerous to count flying quickly towards him." Simon says, "Oh my dreams. Hover left, Hover fast." Rino keeps yelling, "Come on, we escaped being wolf food, I don't want to lose now and become Eagle food. Quickly they're hunting us like prey." They hover quickly towards the Dreamville fields going over Mrs. DreamNot and the ex dream squad chief's little shabby shack. Simon looks back and the Eagles are right on their backs. Simon yells, "Whatever you do Rino, don't look back." Curiosity taking over his senses, Rino looks back and screams, "Oh nightmares." Simon yells, "I said don't look back." They both scream, "Hover even faster." There hover boards pick up speed and they reach the Dreamville fields exiting the sky above the forbidden forest wall just as the birds are beginning to swoop for the kill but they can't pass the edge of the forest wall and bang into each other instead and tumble down into the forbidden forest. They both say, "Slow hover. Hover. Still hover." They look back and watch the spectacle. Rino's sweating and Simon's heart's beating rapidly. Rino says, "I never want to do that again." Simon says, "I hope we won't ever have to do that again." The eagles squawk and make their bird noises to attract prey as Simon and Rino face forward and both say, "Hover forward." They hover in silence to the edge of the Dreamville fields. Simon says, "Hover down." Rino follows Simon and says, "Hover down." They reach the ground and Simon says, "Still hover." Rino says, "Still hover." They look into Dreamville and Rino says, "It's beautiful from here isn't it." Simon says, "Yes. I don't know what to do Rino." Rino says, "What did your dreams tell you to do." Simon says,

"That's it. Thanks Rino. All we have to do is find the ancient passage from Dreamville to the Outsiders world." Rino gasps and says, "Is that all." Simon looks at him. Rino says, "What? I mean, where do we supposedly find this ancient passage?" Simon says, "We need to... we need a new recruit." Rino asks, "And, who is this new ally?" Simon says, "King Régimand DreamRoyal the tenth." Rino says, "Do you think he'll believe us and if he does, will he help us?" Simon looks forward and replies, "He has to, and he's the only one in all of Dreamville who knows anything about the underground passages under DreamRoyal hill, Dreamville and Dream Mountain." Rino says, "Alright, well I guess we better find him." Simon says, "He'll be in his castle. He cancelled school until everyone's found, remember." Just as Simon's finished saying his sentence, his virtual communicator goes off with the virtualcast. The media clown says, "It's a happy Tuesday for few Dreamvillians today. There have been more disturbing reports of missing Dreamvillians. Almont Alldream, the Mayor's son, Simon Dreamlee and Rino DreamScifi have been reported as kidnapped by their hysterical parents and two more gargoyles have also been stolen over night from King DreamRoyal's yard. Oh does anyone have any leads for the dream squad chief and her dream squad cops? If you do, you're urged to report them to them immediately." The virtualcast shuts itself off and Simon looks at Rino. Rino says, "I guess we better go home." Simon says, "No, we can't go home because then we'll have to explain what we did last night and why Almont's missing as well as the others and you said it yourself, if you hadn't of been there, here yourself, you wouldn't believe this story either." Simon goes silent and then continues to say, "No, we definitely can't. The only adult we absolutely have to talk to right now is the King himself." Rino who's looking back at the forbidden forest wall says, "You know I'm with you because right now I want to be anywhere but here." Simon looks at Rino's freaked out expression on his face and looks back to see the wolves shining eyes staring at them from the edge of the woods and the eagles sitting in the tree tops eyeing them. Rino says, "Bone chilling isn't it." Simon says, "Come on. Hover forward." Rino says, "Hover forward." Simon hovers into the closes ancient tree trunk and says, "Cease hover." Rino hovers inside and says, "Cease hover." They step off of their hover boards and Simon says, "We'll have to go on foot from here. Our hover boards should be safe in here until we come back to get them. Follow me." Rino says, "Wait we can hover on the outskirts of Dreamville." Simon says, "No we can't, with so many Dreamvillians missing, the dream squad cops will be patrolling everywhere. No we must leave our hover boards here and remain inconspicuous." After a few moments, Rino agrees, "Alright." They stick their heads out of the ancient tree trunk and survey for any dream squad cop cars. They don't see any and leave the safety of the ancient tree trunk and run towards the shadows of the tall buildings of the Dreamville Films and Movies Production Company on Dreamwood Boulevard.

Silently, they wait in the shadows as they watch a dream security guard walk by. Simon silently signals to Rino to crawl into the thick, green foliage of the rose bushes. They both crawl in the thick, green foliage of the rose bushes and wait for the dream security guard to leave his post for a mid-morning snack break. The dream security guard gets up and walks towards the bush to smell the roses. Simon can smell his blueberry muffin. Simon's stomach rumbles, this tummy rumbling alerts the dream security guard who flashes his flashlight in the rose bush. Simon quietly moves back out of the beam of the flashlight and the security guard says, "Huh... must just be my stomach rumbling." He puts his flashlight back in his pocket and walks to the side door of the building and walks inside. Simon whispers, "Okay now we go." They crawl out of the rose bush and run across the property until they reach another ancient tree trunk. They run inside and catch their breath. Rino says, "Simon here, eat a chocolate bar. I don't want your stomach to get us caught." Simon says, "Thanks Rino." He opens the chocolate bar and devours it as Rino eats a few pieces himself. Rino laughs, "Ha-ha. I never thought I'd be running from tree trunk to tree trunk ever in my life." Simon laughs, "Ha-ah...yeah. Twice now too..." They both stop laughing and get serious again. They run out of the tree trunk, from bush to bush, towards the dream parliamentary building. They hide behind the statues of the ancients to not get caught by the dream security guards and the dream squad cops as they hover by. Simon whispers, "We just need to get to the Hoverway and follow it to the other side of Dreamville and then straight into King DreamRoyal's castle." Rino nods his head in agreement. They step out of the ancient tree trunk and walk right back inside to wait for the dream squad cop to hover by before attempting to resume their quest. The squad cop stops his hover car and steps out of the hover car. He says to his partner, "I never thought about this before but the ancient tree trunks would be great places to hide or even keep kidnap victims tied up and held as hostages." Rino looks at Simon and Simon very softly whispers, "Do you still have your invisibility device?" Rino shakes his head to indicate that he doesn't. He whispers, "I must have dropped it in the forbidden forest wall." They hear the dream squad cops approaching footsteps. Simon puts his hand on Rino's arm and squeezes his invisibility device. The dream squad cops enter the ancient tree trunk and walk all around. Simon and Rino constantly have to keep one step ahead of them so they don't touch the dream squad cops and alert them to their presence. Rino's sweating and Simon's heart's beating fast. The partner, a female dream squad cop remarks, "Strange I think I hear a heart beat but I see nothing in here at all." The male dream squad cop replies, "I see nothing either. You must be hearing your own heart beating." The female dream squad cop says, "Well, we better get back and tell our colleagues to start searching these ancient tree trunks because there's a lot of room in them to hide kidnap victims." The male dream squad cop says, "It's big enough in here to fit a whole family and live comfortably." As they walk out of the ancient tree trunk Rino's foot slips and accidently trips the male dream squad cop. He regains his footing quickly but remains startled as he looks back and says, "I'm tripping on thin air." They walk to their dream squad hover car, climb inside and hover off in the opposite direction of the Hoverway. Simon un-squeezes the invisibility device and says, "Close one." Beads of sweat run down Rino's forehead and he says, "I just about had an anxiety attack which for sure would have gotten us caught." Simon says, "Well we need to calm down and focus. Come on we need to get to the Hoverway." They exit the ancient tree trunk and run in the direction of the Hoverway. For the next two hours, they run towards the Dreamville Hoverway hiding in the bushes when necessary, mostly when hover cars pass by them. They finally reach their first destination.

Standing under the Hoverway, they listen to the calming sound of the Dream Stream River flow underneath the Hoverway. They see the deer drink water; the unicorns drink water, an array of gentle forest animals drink the water. Rino says, "I've never come here before. It's so beautiful." Simon says, "I knew about this place but I've never been here either. It is beautiful." Rino says, "So what's your plan from here Simon?" Simon says, "Do you see those ancient vines underneath the Hoverway." Rino replies, "Yeah, I see them." Simon says, "We're going to climb them and crawl on them all the way around Dreamville until we're by DreamRoyal hill." Rino says, "If you've never been here before, then how did you know about these ancient vines?" Simon replies, "I didn't know about them. What makes you think I did?" Rino's dumbfounded and says, "Huh." Simon says, "Come, we have to start climbing and crawling." Rino says, "This is going to take hours." Simon says, "That's why we have to start getting going, come on." Simon starts to climb an ancient vine, upwards towards the undercarriage of the Hoverway. Rino follows close behind him. They can hear the multiple hover cars, the hover trucks, hover semis, hover vans, and hover buses, all hover above their heads as they reach the top of the ancient vine. They start to crawl along the ancient vine which is really two ancient vines, one grape, the other olive. During their travel, Rino picks grapes and olives, wraps them in the used wrappers of his eaten chocolate bars and puts the packages in his pocket. The sun starts to descend and the daylight hours begin to fade. Simon says, "Rino we've arrived. This is the point where we're the closest to DreamRoyal hill." Rino says, "Simon, the dreamy night time's here. I think we should rest here until morning." Simon replies, "I think your right. This way the gargoyles won't snatch us and turn us into stone statues." Rino says, "What?" Simon decides not to tell Rino about his dream from the last night. Simon says, "Nothing. Don't give yourself an anxiety attack." Simon picks grapes and olives and eats them. Rino also picks grapes and olives and eats them. They fill their stomachs and fall asleep listening to the calming, enchanting flow of the stream way down beneath them. They lie in silence, neither one of them are able to sleep, un-expectantly they hear voices below them. Simon hushes Rino, "Shush…" They look downward, careful not to fall off of the ancient vines and see the gargoyles talking but they can't make out what they're saying. They lift off and fly out of Simon and Rino's view. Rino whispers, "I think we're safe here as long as we need to sleep." Simon nods his head in agreement and says, "Yeah, we should get some sleep." They both lie back down and this time Simon's able to fall to sleep. He dreams of the passages underneath DreamRoyal castle, the tunnels, the ladders, everything he had seen over a year ago but nothing indicates to him which one of these passages is the ancient one that leads to the Outside world accept for one potent clue a quick flash of a golden sun with the image of an ancient DreamRoyal king shaking the hand of what appears to be an Outsider. A song begins to fill his dream.

Truth dreamer, come through ancient passage.
Through the long forgotten, legendary handshake
Of a friendship, now dead
Friendship may never be rekindled but
Wrongs can still be righted
By giving lost ones their freedom
Once again

Chapter Seven – Finding King Dreamroyal And The Ancient Passage

Wednesday morning, Simon opens his eyes, breathes in the fresh, clean air into his lungs and stretches his limbs. He sits up and sees that Rino's nowhere around. He picks some grapes and olives and eats them. Suddenly he gets concerned and says to himself, "What if they took him last night?" Just as his dread began to build inside of him he hears Rino, "Simon, are you up yet?" Simon realizes he's not actually alone and replies, "Yes, and I now realize what you're doing." Rino laughs and says, "Ha-ha. Yeah here's your invisibility device." Simon says, "Thanks." Rino hands it to him. Simon starts down the ancient vine with Rino close behind him. They get to the bottom of the ancient vine and jump off. Simon walks to the Dream Stream River that's as clear as glass and with his hand he scoops up some water and drinks. Rino does the same. In silence they drink until their thirst is quenched and their feeling re-hydrated. Simon sits down and brushes off all the lady bugs that are crawling all over him. Rino says, "So what are we doing today Simon?" Simon replies, "We stick to the plan. We go recruit King DreamRoyal the tenth. We just need to get across this field without getting caught." Rino puts his hand on Simon's shoulder and says, "Well we better go." Simon squeezes his invisibility device and they walk through the field of young, still short, corn plants. They see the hover squad cars going from ancient tree trunk to ancient tree trunk, hoping they find clues or better the kidnapped Dreamvillians. Simon says, "They're absolutely clueless." Rino says, "Totally clueless." They keep walking and reach the bottom of DreamRoyal hill. They walk up the hill and into their beloved king's yard. Simon un-squeezes the invisibility device and they walk up to the castle's front door but before entering Simon turns around and counts the gargoyles, "One, two, three, four, five, six, seven, eight, nine, five of them are guarding Jilla, Dee, Miss

LossDream and Almont." Rino says, "Where?" Simon replies, "I don't know but somewhere in the Outside World." They knock on the door. "Tap, tap, tap, tap…" Simon rings the doorbell, "Ding, Dong, Ding, Ling, Ling, Dong..." Simon says, "Huh, it's in the key of G sharp major." Rino says, "Interesting." Rino leans over and looks in the living room picture window and says, "I don't think he's here Simon." Simon says, "Then we find a way inside and wait for him to come back." They walk around the castle but all the windows are shut and absolutely cannot be opened from the outside. Out of the blue, Rino says, "Simon, they're going to find our hover boards in the ancient tree." Simon says, "Now, is not the time to worry about that." Rino says, "You're right, you're right. Sorry." Simon says, "I need something to pick the lock in order for us to go inside and wait, plus hide." Rino fiddles through his multiple pockets and pulls out a toothpick. Simon grabs it from him and says, "I'll try it." They run to the front of the house and up the stairs. Simon inserts the toothpick into the key hole and the door opens. Rino says, "I can't believe that worked." Simon says, "It didn't. The door was already unlocked." Rino says, "Why would King DreamRoyal leave his castle and not lock the door considering everything that's happening right now in Dreamville?" Simon replies, "Good question, come inside." They illegally enter into their beloved king's castle and Rino shuts and locks the door behind them. Simon sees that the king is clearly not in the media room. Simon goes right into the kitchen and then the dining room but doesn't find the king. Simon goes upstairs and into every room, including the king's prized dreamy study room but doesn't find the king. Simon comes downstairs to find Rino raiding the king's fridge. Simon asks, "Rino, what are you doing?" Rino replies, "We need supplies so I'm packing this backpack I found on the dining room chair over there with fresh fruits, veggies and this container of chocolate cake." Simon says, "Well okay, but if you feel like that backpack is weighing you down at any time, get rid of it." Rino says, "I don't think that'll happen but okay." Simon waits for Rino to finish and says, "Rino, we have to go without the king." Rino asks, "Go where?" Simon says, "I'm not sure yet. Follow me." Rino follows Simon into the king's basement.

Once in the basement, Simon points at the open secret trap door. Rino says, "Should we go down there?" Simon says without hesitation, "Absolutely." Rino starts down the ladder and then Simon starts down as well but he closes the trap door and with the string, pulls the carpet over the door. They descend downward into the secret science laboratory. Simon gets off of the ladder, steps onto the cement floor and turns around.

Rino already turned on the ancient lights and holds up a glass container containing sparkly silver dust. Rino says, "I think this silver dust might neutralize the golden dust's effects but, of course, I can't really test out my hypothesis." Simon says, "I'll trust your instincts. Put it in your back pack." Rino places the glass container in his back pack. Simon looks around the room and says, "I wonder if there's anything else in here that we could use?" He looks around and sees nothing else of use. Simon says, "I don't think there's anything else here we can use." They walk down the long corridor with the ancient painted portraits of the DreamRoyal family. Rino follows Simon into the tunnel past the many rooms, past the rooms with the jewels, gems and diamonds and leads them into the large room with the multiple ladders leading to the surface. Simon says, "We can't go up this one because we already know it leads to the dream squad station." Rino says, "Which one do we go up then?" Simon says, "I'm not sure. We'll have to try them all." Rino starts to climb a ladder, and Simon climbs a different one. Rino opens the trap door and quickly closes it, he yells, "This door opens into Dreamtrue School." Simon opens his trap door and quickly closes it, he says, "This one opens in the parliamentary building." Rino had climbed a second ladder and opens a second trap door. He quickly closes it and says, "This one opens in the Dreamville Mall." Simon climbed and already opened another trap door, says, "This one opens in the office of Mr. MakesFilmDreams. He's a great guy." Rino says, "This is going to take forever." Simon says, "You're right. Look for a trap door with the image of a sun and inside the sun is an ancient royal shaking the hand of an outsider peasant." Rino says, "None of the trap doors have a picture like that Simon." Simon climbs down the ladder and says, "None of these ladders are the ancient passage to the Outside World." Rino says, "Well we can't be sure unless we check them all." They look around the large room and Simon says, "There must be hundreds of trap doors." All of a sudden, a voice says, "There are three hundred and seventy-two trap doors to be exact." Simon and Almont turn around and see the new dream squad chief and the dream squad cops standing in the center of the room. She continues to say, "Where have you boys been? And, if you two are here, where are your friends and Miss LossDream?" Simon replies, "We don't know." Rino replies, "That's what we're trying to figure out." She says, "Well, very well then, bring them in boys." Simon says, "What? What reasons?" She says, "What for? For giving your parents heart break, that's what for. You both should be ashamed of yourselves running away when there are legitimately kidnapped Dreamvillians out there somewhere. I knew you two were around somewhere when we found your hover boards in the ancient tree just outside of the forbidden forest wall." Simon says, "But we're trying to find them just like you." Simon takes his invisibility device out of his pocket and squeezes it. He disappears. He runs towards Rino and touches his arm. He says, "Quick trip them." Rino trips and pushes the dream squad cops who are confused and disoriented by the invisible duo. They run out of the large room into the passage to the rock wall where they lean against the wall and watch as the dream squad and the new female chief run past them. The dream squad chief yells, "Quickly, this is some kind of trick, we'll find them." Simon and Rino wait until they no longer hear their footsteps or even the echo of their footsteps before speaking. Simon un-squeezes the invisibility device and takes his hand off of Rino's arm. Simon says, "We need to find that image I told you about earlier." Rino says, "Okay. It sure would help if we knew where King DreamRoyal is to get his expertise regarding these underground corridors, tunnels, secret rooms and this so called ancient passage way." Simon turns around and looks at the rock wall, he says, "Rino, do you realize which wall this is?" Rino says, "A rock wall. Is it the stone wall? It's hard to tell when practically all the walls are rock." Simon taps the stone wall three times. The stone wall opens and they walk inside the looking window room. The stone wall closes behind them. Simon claps his hands and the lights come on. Simon sees the ancient book they had discovered the first time he was in this room open to a page with a picture of the image he was previously explaining to Rino. Simon excitedly says, "Rino, look in this book at this image. This is the image from my dream. This is the image we need to find and it will lead us to the ancient passage to the Outside world." Rino approaches the book and looks at the image. He reads out loud the caption at the bottom of the page, "On this Thursday of the year thirteen thirty-eight, may peace, prosperity and trust reign between Dreamvillians of Dreamville and humans of the Outside world. Symbolized by King Régimand DreamRoyal the third and Master MagicDream's hand shake." Simon says, "So it's not a human in this picture like I originally thought but the image of Master MagicDream himself." Rino says, "Well it's nice to put a face to the name." Rino walks to the red velvet curtains and opens them. They look out the looking window into the Outside world. Rino says, "Can it be? It's night time already." Simon says, "It looks that way and we've accomplished nothing." A soft male voice says, "Not nothing, turn around." Simon and Rino turn around and see nothing. Rino turns to Simon and says, "Did you say that?" Simon shakes his head and says, "No, I thought maybe you did." Suddenly, a ghostly figure appears before them. Simon says, "A ghost. I mean, are you a ghost?" The ghost says, "I am and you'll find many like me in here since you Simon Dreamlee, the truth dreamer saved King DreamRoyal's dreams." Rino says, "Whoa, wait one minute. Let me wrap my mind around this." The ghost laughs and says, "Look at the science inclined dreamer, can't understand what can't be concretely explained by theories and science projects. I'm a real ghost Rino DreamScifi, the skeptic." Rino asks, "Then who are you?" The ghost replies, "I'm the ghost of King DreamRoyal the third." Simon asks, "Why did you call me truth dreamer?" The ghost of King DreamRoyal third replies, "Because that is your gift Simon and a great gift at that." Simon says, "I just realized something. I never needed King DreamRoyal the tenth; it's you I need, you, King DreamRoyal the third." Rino who's insulted by the skeptic comment says, "It is?" Simon says, "You must lead us down the ancient passage to the Outside world." The ghost of King DreamRoyal the third says, "Precisely, follow me." He floats through the stone wall. Rino rolls his eyes and sarcastically says, "Oh this ought to be easy." Simon taps the wall and the stone wall opens, they walk out into the passage and the stone wall closes behind them. The ghost of DreamRoyal the third says, "Sometimes I forget that I'm a ghost but come along." They follow the floating ghost down the other side of the large room with the ladders into a passage they had not yet seen. This passage is filled with painted portraits of Dreamville from decade to decade. Rino comments, "Wow, Dreamville has really evolved." The ghost of King DreamRoyal the third says, "Yes indeed, although Dreamville has always been the place of dreams and dreams come true, there have been some definite improvements over the centuries." Rino says, "Ah yeah, I see that." Simon says, "Are we in the ancient passage?" The ghost replies, "We're in an ancient passage." Simon asks, "But is it the one to the outside world?" The ghost replies, "No, we're not there yet. Just follow me." They follow the ghost of King DreamRoyal the third down the corridor until they reach an opening, not necessarily a room at least, construction seemingly was never completed.

Simon and Rino look around at the dimly lit room with tree roots on the walls and trickling drops of water from the ceiling. Simon asks, "King DreamRoyal the third, where have you brought us?" The ghost replies, "Simon, this is the ancient passage." Rino remarks, "This, this is the ancient passage." The ghost says, "Yeah, I know you were expecting something grander, well maintained, lined in gold, well, it's not." Simon says, "Obviously." The ghost says, "Follow me." They follow the ghost into the wide opening that seems more like a giant hole in the ground. Simon asks, "How large is this place." The ghost replies, "It held over five thousand Dreamvillians, the whole population, at one time but that time has passed." Simon says, "So Dreamvillians once knew about this location?" The ghost replies, "Once but it's never been used since the…" The ghost stops talking. Rino asks, "Since the what?" Simon says, "Yeah, since the what?" Their questions get interrupted by the flash light of someone or something walking towards them. Simon asks, "Who's there. Who or what are you?" Suddenly, they can make out the face. Simon says, "Milany." Milany replies, "Sire, we've got to hurry." The ghost king says, "Okay, everyone, follow me, this way now." Rino whispers, "Milany?" Simon whispers, "Milany is the ghost of this ghost king's servant." Milany says, "I will serve you too Simon Dreamlee." Simon says, "There's no need for that but thanks." The ghost king hushes everyone, "Shush we're approaching the ancient access to the outside world." Milany hushes everyone, "Shush, we must speak quietly." They follow the ghost right up to the back of a water fall. They can see right into the night through the water fall. They see an outsiders' city highlighted by their streetlights and the faint lights of stars through the thick smog. They see their gasoline vehicles, stores, gas stations, restaurants, sky scrapers, buildings, banks and more smog. Rino says, "This whole time the Outsider's can see us and can come into Dreamville through this secret access." The ghost of King DreamRoyal the third says, "No, they cannot hear us or see us or come through this access because it is very well camouflaged on their side for our protection." Simon asks, "Camouflaged how?" The ghost king says, "First things first, spread that silvery, sparkly grey dust on yourselves so on you." Rino takes out the container but hesitates and says, "How are we supposed to know that you're not trying to trick us and turn us into who knows what." Simon says, "I think that if they were trying to trick us or trap us, they would have already done so." The ghost king says, "That's fine, okay, Rino's nature's to be a skeptic. Go ahead Rino spread the dust on me." Rino opens the jar, takes the jar and shakes some dust out onto the ghost king. They wait a couple moments to see what happens. Nothing happens. Rino says, "Of course nothing going to happen to you, you're a ghost." Simon says, "What does the silvery dust do?" The ghost says you'll know when the time comes." Rino says, "What kind of answer is that?" The ghost says, "You should go now and be protected through the cover of darkness and make sure to hide during the daylight hours." Rino asks, "Aren't you coming with us?"

The ghost king replies, "No, I'm afraid I do not exist past this water fall. You must rescue your friends yourselves." Simon asks, "But how are we to know where to look?" The ghost replies, "Simon, little truth dreamer, follow your dream come true to the beginning where it all began." Simon says, "Follow my dream come true." Simon and Rino look at each other and walk through the water fall. Rino says, "Hey, I'm not getting wet." Simon lifts his hands up and tries to feel the water, he says, "I'm not getting wet either." Rino says, "It's an illusion." It takes them, Rino and Simon ten minutes to walk through the water fall before they reach the other side, the outside world. They both step out of the water fall and into a cemetery with statues, headstones, graves and a large structure, a church. Rino asks, "What is this place?" Simon says, "The Outsiders place of rest when their lives are over on earth." Rino turns towards to where the water fall should be and says, "Simon, where did it go?" Simon turns around and says, "I don't know." They both hold their hands out but in place of the water fall is nothing but a rock wall with a graffiti drawing, intricately painted on its surface. Simon says, "Look at these paintings. They're exact images of the gargoyles, right down to the most intricate details and some other strange creatures I've never seen before. Have you ever seen these before Rino?" Rino takes a look and says, "No, never." Simon reads the signature of the graffiti artist out loud, "Diana Crow, this girl's the artist and she's drawn these images." He studies the images of the strange creatures and whispers, "Chimeras." Rino says, "What?" Simon says, "Ah nothing. We better walk around to try and locate our friends." Rino says, "Yeah right, how are we supposed to do that?" Simon says, "Rino, watch for the gargoyles in the air." Simon reads the names on the tombstones and sees the name of Master MagicDream. He sees the phony, man-made statues of gargoyles and the phony statues of chimeras. Rino waits for Simon at the entrance into the graveyard. Simon walks up to him and they step out into the Outsiders cement streets. Rino says, "This place is odd, almost…" Simon says, "Cold." Rino says, "Not quite, it's got an appeal, a charm but there's something missing." Simon says, "Dreams." Rino says, "Yes, that's it, it lacks dreams, the colors of dreams. Everything's grey, charcoal and black." Simon says, "I agree." Rino asks, "So where to Simon?" Rino's silent, looks into the night sky and waits for Simon's response to his question when they hear the sound of a car door slam. A man yells, "Hey you there. Get out of there you hooligan vandals." Simon says, "Run." Rino follows Simon as they run into a back alley, through the back alley and out the other end. Their run is not over as the cemetery grounds caretaker catches up to them in his gasoline powered car. He shines his lights on them. He yells, "You there, stop." Simon and Rino start to run down the poorly lit street of closed shops, through parked vehicles and into the entrance of one of the buildings. They watch the man drive by the building and turn right onto another street. They hear him yell, "One of these nights, I'll catch you vandalizing my cemetery and when I do, you'll be disciplined severely. The parishioners are not going to put up with you criminals any longer." Simon and Rino look at each other with fear in both their eyes. Simon says, "We've got to find our friends, and fast." Rino says, "Yeah before the crazy human guy finds us first." Simon says, "Yeah I mean what's so wrong with this so called vandalism guy anyway?" Simon sticks his head out of the entrance and continues to say, "Okay it looks like he's not around anymore and we can't stay here." They exit the entrance and walk back out onto the sidewalk.

They walk down the sidewalk past the vehicles to their left and a variety of buildings to their right. Rino says, "Hey look Simon, they name their streets too just like in Dreamville only they don't use the word dream in their street names. We're on Main Street. I wonder what street that cemetery was on so we know how to get back there." Simon says, "Well that sign says Cemetery Street." Rino says, "That must be the street we'll have to find in order to get back to Dreamville." Simon nods his head and says, "Right now, that's the very least of my concerns." Rino says, "Ah, Oh, you're right. Sorry. It's just that I miss Dreamville." Simon says, "I do too Rino. I do too." They walk down another street going the opposite direction of Cemetery Street. Simon says, "Okay we're on Principal Street." Rino pulls out his virtual communicator and exclaims, "Our technology still functions in this world." Simon pulls out his virtual communicator and starts entering the street names and forming a map of the very well evolved Outsiders city. Simon says, "I'll make a map." Rino says, "Great idea. I'm going to try and virtually communicate with Dee." Rino's says, "Dee, come in Dee." Rino sighs and says, "Nothing." All of a sudden, they un-expectantly hear, Jilla's voice, "Simon, come in Simon." Simon opens his virtual communicator and Jilla's image streams, Simon says, "Jilla I'm here. Can you tell me where you are?" Jilla replies, "Simon, we've been kidnapped by the gargoyles, Almont, Miss LossDream, me and for some unexplainable reason Rino's new girlfriend Dee." Simon says, "I know that Jilla, try and put your jealousy aside for now and describe to me your surroundings." Almont grabs the virtual communicator and says, "Simon, ah dude, so great to hear your voice again." Simon says, "Guys, you're running out of time. Describe to me your surroundings." Simon looks up and sees the sun starting to rise, he looks back down at the virtual images of his friends and Almont says, "We're in some kind of room, it's pleasant but dark. I remember walking down a long hallway to get into this room. I think we're in a mansion of some kind with lots of Master MagicDream's magical creations. That's all I've got Simon." Jilla says, "Sorry Simon but I was knocked out by weird golden dust when they took me and I woke up in this room." Rino says, "Jilla what's happening to your hand. They watch as their friends turn into stone statues and the virtual communication gets cut off. Simon looks up and says, "The suns up, it's Thursday morning. We better hide." Rino says, "Where? There's no trees, or bushes that are dense enough to hide in either." Simon says, "We have a little while before the street fills with Outsiders so, we look for cover." They walk past a white van with an advertising sign painted on the side saying magic vacuum cleaner, the van door opens and two people grab both Simon and Rino, blindfold them and tie their hands before either of them can get a look at their human kidnappers.

Chapter Eight – Simon And Rino's Kidnappers

Captives they struggle to get their hands free and their blindfolds off but to no avail. They can still talk because their mouths have not been gagged. Simon and Rino hear the van start and can feel the van driving along the humans, Outsiders, cement yet ruff streets. Simon risks speaking and asks, "Who are you?" No one responds. Simon asks another question, "Why have you kidnapped us?" Still no one answers, he hears Rino struggling to get his hands free. Rino says, "Oh un-dreamy dreams, my feet are tied up too." Simon tries to move his feet and says, "So are mine." Rino loudly asks, "Answer him... Why? Who are you?" The two humans still don't answer them. Simon asks, "What's with the silent treatment? If you didn't want us to talk you would have gagged our mouths but you didn't." Finally, a female voice says, "Keep it down back there or you'll draw attention to us." Simon says, "No, no I'll not keep it down until you tell me who you are." The female voice replies, "Okay, Okay..." The male voice says, "No, not yet. Wait until we get there." Simon says, "No tell me. And, get where?" The female voice says to the male voice, "I have to say something. Simon Dreamlee..." Simon says, "How do you know my name?" The female voice laughs very gently and says, "Ha-ha. One question at a time Simon, first, I'm Diana." Rino says, "The girl graffiti artist from the cemetery?" Diana replies, "No, I'm her great grand-daughter." Simon says, "Okay great. Why have you kidnapped us?" Diana replies, "He couldn't think of another way to explain to you why you need to come with us for your own protection." Simon says, "Really, maybe just talking to us." Diana says, "We couldn't risk it, seeing how so far along you Dreamvillians are technologically." Simon says, "We're not murderers if that's what you're afraid of." Diana says, "I'm not sure that's what we're afraid of, I'm just doing what I was told do." Simon says, "Okay so you've come to help us, well, then please un-tie us." Diana says, "Not yet, we have to get you two inside before the sun here in our world burns your eyes." Rino says, "What?" Diana says, "There's so much pollution in our world that the ozone layer is so depleted that your kind is not safe in direct sunlight." They feel the van turn and stop. The van's motor stops running and Diana says, "We're here and you'll be safe, at least, for during the daylight hours." They hear the two front doors open and close. Rino says, "Hey, you can't just leave us like this." They hear the sliding door open and feel blankets being draped over them as they're guided inside a building. Diana takes the blanket off of Simon and then Rino. The male takes Rino's blindfold off and says, "I'm Justin." Rino says, "I'm Rino." Diana takes Simon's blindfold off and says, "Nice to meet you Simon Dreamlee." Simon feels like he's looking upon pure beauty. Diana, also thirteen, is mostly brunette, highlighted by streaks of red, bronze and blond. She has emerald green eyes and is the perfect height for him. Simon says, "Ah…yeah… Nice to see, ah…meet you too Diana." Diana says, "This is my brother Justin." Simon says, "Nice to meet you Justin." Justin says, "We're the MagicDream's." Simon says, "You're the direct descendants." Diana says, "Yes but not in this world. We were saved by this human family from the mob that wants to burn down our inheritance, the mansion. They say it's evil." Simon hangs on every word Diana says, he says, "How are you not affected by the sun?" Justin replies, "We've adapted or evolved to the climate in this world because of our exposure to it from birth." Rino says, "Classic proof, you're both living proof of the theory of adaptability." Simon says, "Okay well, this has been great, but Rino and I have to get going." Diana says, "Here wear these, there called sunglasses." Justin says, "Wear these also sun block and a baseball cap." Simon and Rino slather the sun block on their exposed arms, legs, feet, hands and face. They put the sunglasses on as well. Simon and Rino open the front door of the house and step out of the house. Diana says, "Wait you don't think we'll let you go by yourselves do you?" Justin says, "Yeah we can show you how to get to the mansion." Simon looks at Rino and then he looks at Diana, he says, "I don't want you to get hurt." Diana says, "Nonsense, we may have been born in this world but we still feel strong ties to Dreamville. I don't care if I get hurt and you're not talking me out of helping you." Diana stands besides Simon who's impressed with her determination and braveness. Simon smiles at her and she smiles back. Rino says, "Okay we should go." Simon says, "Lead the way Diana." Rino says, "We can take the van." Justin replies, "Actually, technically, I can't really drive it legally. I'm only fifteen and Diana's only thirteen. I kind of stole the van last night to find you guys and I'm happy we did." Simon says, "You stole the van?" Justin says, "Well more like borrowed it, it's my adoptive father's van but boy when he sees me next he'll be pretty peeved." Rino says, "So you risked getting arrested just to help us." Justin says, "Every night since this whole ordeal started a week ago." Simon and Rino look at each other and Simon says, "Thanks." Rino says, "Yeah thank you." Simon suddenly looks at his hand and says, "Ah." Diana takes the bottle of sun block and rubs some on his hand. Diana says, "Here put this in your back pack and she hands the bottle to Rino who places it in his back pack. They start walking on the sidewalk. Simon enters the street name, Tulip Drive. They walk onto Sunset boulevard and then unto River Street. Rino says, "We've been walking for over an hour now. Where's this mansion." Justin replies, "On foot, another two hours away." Diana says, "Quick hide in here." They follow her down into a ditch and into a culvert. Simon asks, "Why are we hiding." Justin says, "The cops are looking for us. We kind of stole the van and technically in this world we're considered runaways." Simon and Rino laugh, "Ha-ha." Simon says, "That's funny because we're considered runaways in Dreamville too. You know there probably are a lot of similarities between both our worlds." Rino says, "Listen." They hear sirens from the police cars and police officers talking over their radios, "Yeah, the cemetery caretaker swears he saw them last night vandalizing the graveyard. They've got to be around there somewhere." The police officer driving the police car says, "Roger that, we'll head there now." The police car drives off in the direction of the cemetery. Justin says, "Good they think we're there and we'll be going in the opposite direction." Simon says, "Okay, well, is there a way we can stick to these, whatever these are." Diana says, "This is a culvert and yes I think we can."

They travel by the culverts and Simon asks continuously what street they're under so he can fill in his map. Rino tensely says, "What is that? Sounds like wolves. Oh my un-dreamy dreams, the wolves have found us." Diana says, Relax we're passing the dog pound. Simon asks, "Dog pound?" Diana says, "Yes when people get tired of their dogs or can no longer afford to take care of them, they end up here. Eventually, if no one wants them, they kill them." Justin says, "The saddest cases are when the owners die before their pets and don't make arrangements for someone to take care of their pets once they're deceased." Rino says, "That's terrible." Simon says, "Terrible, but it gives me an idea. I have an idea to occupy the police." Simon climbs up the ditch and walks across the street. The rest follow behind him. Simon walks up to the gate and unhooks the latch, releasing all the captive dogs. Simon says, "Quick get back in the ditch." Diana says, "Why did you do that?" Simon says, "Because now the police will have to catch the dogs before even thinking of catching us." Justin says, "Not necessarily, they have dog catchers in this world." Diana says, "No well, with that many dogs loose, the police will have to help them. Good idea Simon." They get back in the ditch and travel by culverts to a street called Prune Drive. Justin says, "There's no more culverts passed this point. We have to travel by foot on the sidewalks." Simon says, "We should be safe from here on." Diana says, "Not really, we have to pass the police station to get to the mansion." They run up to the police station and along side of the building as the police cars keep coming out of the parking lot. They hear a patrol car's police radio, "Multiple dogs got loose from the pound, we need every cop on this one until all dogs are caught, I repeat until all dogs are caught." Rino looks at Simon and the two high five each other. Simon whispers, "Wait until they're all gone and then we'll be able to walk on the sidewalk freely." They watch the police cars going in the opposite direction from their destination. They listen to the dogs running the other way. "Woof... Woof... Woof..." Justin leads the way while Simon and Diana walk side by side. Diana says to Simon, "For your map, we're walking on Grocer Boulevard and this one coming up is Stratford drive." Simon keeps building his map of the Outsiders city. Simon asks, "What's the name of this city?" Diana says, "You're in Newsprings city, city of magic." Simon says, 'City of magic?" Diana says, "Yes when my ancestor Master MagicDream, his wife and four children came from Dreamville, he bravely opened a magic shop. He even organized magic shows to entertain the humans. Justin says, "He made himself the headliner too in his shows." Diana says, "Of course, he couldn't reveal too much magic to the humans all at once or else they'd have burnt him for being a wizard but he thrived and became rich." Justin says, "He passed on his knowledge to his children who passed it on to their children and so on." Rino says, "That makes you two half human and half Dreamvillian." Justin says, "We're certainly many generations removed from being Dreamvillians but we still feel that connection." Simon and Diana look at each other, Simon says, "I feel the connection between us too." Diana smiles at Simon. Rino says, "Act casual, there's a police car coming this way." They get into a circle and pretend to have a conversation as the police officer just drives by without noticing them. Justin says, "We're here." Rino says, "Here where? It just looks like broken down buildings." Simon looks around and sees the mansion. He says, "Is that it over there?" Diana says, "Yes it is. That's supposed to be our house, our inheritance but the new police chief has convinced humans that it's evil, that magic's evil." Simon says, "That's terrible. That's like having your dreams stolen." Diana says, "It is but we can't even make them relate to that because most of these humans don't really have dreams, many chose not to dream at all even though they're capable." Simon says, "They choose not to dream so they don't have nightmares." Diana says, "My family and our gift for magic were providing them ideas for their imaginations and relief from their everyday lives." Justin interrupts and says, "Are we going inside or what?" Simon says, "Definitely, we have no other choice." They walk up the quarter mile long driveway and up the steps. Simon stops and everyone looks at him, Diana asks, "What's wrong Simon?" Simon looks around and says, "This is too simple." Rino asks, "What do you mean?" Simon replies, "I mean, sure we go in we look through the whole house and hopefully eventually find our friends during the day when the gargoyles are statues. But, what about night time again?" Rino says, "He's right, they'll just kidnap them again or if not them other Dreamvillians until they get what they want in return." Simon says, "Exactly, we have to wait for the gargoyles and ask them what they want in order to stop kidnapping Dreamvillians." Justin says, "Oh I see, so it's not as simple as finding them and then going back home." Simon says, "No it's not." They see a police car go by the end of the driveway and Simon says, "We should go inside now though." Justin fiddles with the loose door handle and opens the door. All four of them walk inside the large mansion. Justin closes the door behind him and says, "Well here we are." Simon asks, "How do you know we needed to come here?" Diana says, "Because we have been observing the gargoyles just like you Simon." Simon says, "Okay, we should stay together and look for a door with a picture of the sun and in the center, your ancestor shaking hands with our ancient king from the thirteen hundreds." Justin says, "Okay." Rino says, "Sure thing." Diana says, "Okay." They walk out of the foyer into a large living room with an eclectic array of furniture from many different decades and centuries. Simon says, "We're also looking for a corridor with strange objects, probably, used by your ancestors in their ancient magic shows." Diana shrugs her shoulders and Justin says, "I don't know." Rino says, "You lived here and you don't know." Diana says, "Yes we lived here but we don't know all its secrets." Rino says, "Its?" Diana says, "This house, we don't know every little detail and secret passage." Justin says, "In fact, we don't know of any." Simon says, "Well we're about to discover them." They follow Simon, he says, "Large dining room with four chandeliers ordained with crystals. This isn't it." They follow out of the Dining room and into another room, Simon says, "Large study with multiple books about magic written by Master MagicDream himself from the time after his departure from Dreamville. This isn't it either" They walk out of the study and into the large kitchen of white cabinetry with glass doors displaying beautiful antique dishes from multiple parts of the Outsiders world. Simon says, "This isn't it either." Simon says, "We need to go upstairs." Justin says, "Well there's stairs right behind you to go upstairs. If we need to come back downstairs, we can come back down the one's that lead into the foyer and the main entrance." Simon starts walking upstairs and the others follow him.

Once in the hallway, Simon says, "This is closer to my dream, but not quite." His virtual communicator goes off and Almont streams, "Simon, come in, Simon are you there?" Simon takes out his virtual communicator from his pocket and he replies, "I'm here Almont." Rino looks at his virtual communicator and says, "It's ten, still early evening." Simon says, "Almont, the gargoyles aren't awake yet are they?" Almont replies, "No they wake up after midnight." Simon asks, "How many of you are awake?" Almont replies, "All of us." Simon says, "Good, we're in the mansion where you're all being held captive. You have to make a lot of noise to help us so we can find you." Almont turns to everyone and says, "Did you hear that Jilla, Dee... Miss LossDream? What about you King DreamRoyal?" They all echo back, "We heard." They start banging on the walls. Simon says, "Wait King DreamRoyal's there with you?" Almont says, "Yeah they kidnapped him last night and brought him here." Rino says, "Listen, I hear them." Simon says, "Excellent, keep banging you guys, we'll find you. Sign out." He puts his virtual communicator in his pocket. Diana follows alongside of Simon while Rino and Justin listen to the walls as they get closer to the sounds of the banging. They reach the other end of the hall. Rino says, "It's no use, the banging sounds like it's coming from everywhere, every wall." Simon says, "Or from down below." Simon looks at Diana, and asks, "Is there a basement in this mansion?" Diana nods her head and says, "Yes there is, follow me." Simon says, "Quickly, the gargoyles wake up at midnight." They run downstairs into the foyer and from the foyer they run down the stairs to the dark basement.

Once in the basement, Simon says, "Where are the lights." Justin turns the lights on and says, "Does this resemble your dream?" Simon says, "No but it doesn't matter because listen, there banging is really close." Rino listens to the walls and says, "They're down here somewhere." Simon opens all doors as he walks along the long, large basement and sees the images that Almont was describing in his dream. Simon says, "We're on the right track." He opens the last door and stares inside. Rino says, "It's still no use, they're loud down here but I can't find anything to indicate they're here." Simon says, "They're here Rino. Look." Rino looks in the room and sees the picture of the sun with the image of the two ancient men shaking hands. Rino says, "Oh my dreams. It's true." Simon walks towards the wall with Diana by his side, he taps the wall the same way Lionessa tapped the wall in his dream, the wall opens. They stare at the wall opening and listen to their friends banging cease. Jilla, Almont, Miss LossDream and King DreamRoyal come running out of the room. Dee screams, "Rino, you came to rescue me." Rino looks at Jilla just as Dee smooches him. Rino says, "Ah yeah I came to rescue you." Almont stands in front of Jilla to block her view of the lovebird reunion. Jilla says, "Oh Simon you came to rescue me." Jilla kisses Simon on the cheek. Simon says, "Actually, I came to rescue everyone. Almont here's the one who came to rescue you. He purposely got himself kidnapped just so we could find you." Jilla looks at Almont and kisses him on the cheek too. Almont blushes, but at the same time, she can't help but see Dee and her ex-boyfriend Rino smooch. She walks up to them and slaps Rino on the left cheek. Rino puts his hand to his cheek and says, "I deserve that." Jilla says, "I'm happy you agree because I now feel better. He's all yours Dee." Almont looks at his virtual communicator and grabs Jilla's hand, he says, "Look everyone, we've got five minutes to get out of here before, Lionessa, Gargantua, Martua, Wolverina and Snakerina wake up to keep us from escaping." Rino takes Dee's hand and everyone, Dee and Rino, King DreamRoyal and Miss LossDream, Almont and Jilla, Justin, Simon and Diana, runs out of the room into the main corridor of the basement, upstairs to the first floor and out the front door of the mansion in less than four minutes.

Once outside, Simon says, "Over here, in this shed. We have to hide." They all run to the shed and get inside. Simon shuts the door and observes the mansion from the small windows. Almont says, "What's your plan Simon?" Simon replies, "Everyone will stay in here when the gargoyles come out and the others get here. No matter what you all stay in here and don't reveal yourselves, I'm going to go out there and talk to them. I need to find out what they want from us Dreamvillians." Rino whispers "Look." Almont, Simon and Rino as well as the others see the five gargoyles come out of the mansion. Almont whispers, "No way, I'm letting you go out there alone." Jilla whispers, "Me neither, we're friends and friends don't turn their backs on each other in times of crisis." Simon whispers, "Look you guys, I rather be alone, because whatever they want, it has to do with something with me according to my dreams, they think I'm some sort of truth dreamer." King DreamRoyal coughs rather loudly which opens his long, large black robe for everyone to see that he's wearing royal gems around his neck. He quickly closes his robe. They see the gargoyles coming towards the shed. Simon whispers, "Everyone, get down to the floor." They hear the gargoyles heavy steps walking all around the shed but they just as quickly walk away when they hear a car pull into the yard. Diana whispers, "Someone's here, if they see the living, breathing gargoyles, they'll kill them." Simon, who's face to face with Diana, sees the genuine care in her eyes; he decides to risk getting up and looks out the small window to see a police car in the front yard. He whispers, "It's a police car but there's no sign of anyone, not even the gargoyles." He sees the front door is wide open as the light from the mansion lights up the front yard, Simon whispers, "I'm going out there. No matter what happens, everyone stays in here." Simon waits for their answers, Diana and Justin say, "Sure Simon." King DreamRoyal and Miss LossDream say, "Sure Simon." Rino and Dee say, "Alright." Jilla and Almont say nothing. Simon waits a little longer and whispers, "Jilla, Almont, you two better stay in here." Simon opens the shed door, walks out of the shed, closes the shed door and looks around the yard, he sees nothing. He hears nothing either. He walks up to the side of the steps and leans over the steps to look in the mansion. He sees the five gargoyles talking to someone, he can't see who, but he looks at the floor and he can make out human shoes amongst the large gargoyle feet and their claws. Suddenly, he hears the other gargoyles wings flying down from out of the night sky. All remaining nine gargoyles are landing in the front yard. Simon hides in the shadows of the grand steps as he watches the wonderfully scary spectacle. He grows confused with what he has just witnessed and wishes he could hear the conversation between the two human police officers and the five gargoyles in the mansion because mysteriously, nothing makes sense to him anymore. This wasn't part of his dreams. There weren't human police in cahoots with the gargoyles. He leans in but stays successfully in the shadows to try and hear their conversation. The other nine gargoyles enter into the house which renews the loud but indiscernible conversation. Luckily, none of them close the front door.

Chapter Nine – The Return

Simon waits in the shadows when suddenly the conversation grows into yelling. Gargantua yells, "Well what do you expect us to do? They escaped." The female voice of the human police officer yells back, "You will figure out what to do or your friends are dead." Lionessa yells, "You can't kill them, you just can't." Sartua loudly says with a slight slither, "Look, we'll find them and bring them to you just don't hurt any of our friends." Gargantua asks, "You still promise not to hurt the Dreamvillians right?" The male voice of the other human police officer says, "Of course, we have no use for hurting them we just need them to get back what's ours." Simon can't help thinking the voices sound familiar but can't be a hundred percent sure unless he sees their faces. Gargantua says, "Well you heard them, spread out and find them escapees and anyone else that might be with them. We have to catch them before they get back to Dreamville." Simon gets a huge gust of wind as all fourteen gargoyles fly out of the mansion and into the night sky to find their escapees including him. Thankfully, they're still all in the shed. Simon leans his head to see inside and just about gets caught by the male police officer as he turns his head. Simon quickly leans back into the shadows. The two human police officers walk out of the mansion. The female voice says, "We need them as collateral to get what we want. Absolutely, those gargoyles have to get them back, if not, their friends and them are dead. I don't care." The male voice says, "It won't come to that. It shouldn't come to that. I hope it won't come to that. I don't want anyone to die." The female voice says, "Shut up you spineless excuse for a being." They walk to the police car and get inside. Simon wants to see their faces but he can't risk coming out of the shadows. The police car drives off and turns left out of the driveway. Simon looks up in the sky and on all the surrounding buildings to see if there are any gargoyles, he sees none. He comes out of the shadows and runs to the shed. He opens the door and walks inside. He closes the door behind him and looks at everyone. They all stop chewing on the food from Rino's back pack and look at Simon. They all wait in silence for him to tell them what he saw.

Simon whispers, "The two human police officers are in cahoots with the living, breathing gargoyles." Jilla, who's not eating anything, whispers, "Yes and…" Simon whispers, "The gargoyles have to find us in order for the two police officers to give them back their friends alive and not murdered." Almont, who's also not eating anything, whispers, "Yes and…" Simon whispers, "The gargoyles are being blackmailed into kidnapping you guys by these two human police officers so I think we should reveal ourselves to them and tell them that we'll help them out to defeat these two evil hearted humans." Jilla whispers, "Great idea. But, did you see who are the two, supposedly, human police officers?" Simon looks at Jilla and whispers, "No, I couldn't risk leaning out of the shadows or they would have caught me for sure." Almont whispers, "Simon, Jilla and I saw their faces." Simon whispers, "Okay and…" Jilla says, "It's Miss DreamNot and the ex-dream squad chief." Simon whispers, "I thought their voices sounded familiar. But, how… how did they get jobs as police officers in the Outside world?" Diana whispers, "They took over when our police chief went missing. They said they received word from one of their superior officers to come here and chief our police staff until our actual chief's found." Jilla says, "They kidnapped their police chief too." King DreamRoyal the tenth says, "There's no question in my mind anymore that Miss DreamNot is pure evil." Almont whispers, "So is the ex dream squad chief for going along with her ill-omened plots." They all look at Simon and Almont asks, "Well Simon, how do we foil her wicked plot this time around?" Simon replies, "I'm thinking." No one noticed they were gradually using their normal tones of voice instead of whispering, at this point, the shed door gets ripped off and Gargantua and the other gargoyles stand between them and escaping. They all freeze at the sight of the tall gargoyles as they get captured. Simon says, "Wait, whatever you need we can get for you." Gargantua grabs Simon and says, "That's right you can if we bring you to Miss DreamNot." Simon says, "No really Gargantua. What do you want from us in exchange for not bringing us to Miss DreamNot?" Gargantua signals his fellow gargoyles to release their grips on the Dreamvillians, he asks, "What are you offering to do for us?" Simon says, "I'm offering to help you get your friends back alive and confronting Miss DreamNot all together as a united front." Sartua says, "Gargantua, just stick to their demands." Gargantua says, "No wait, we should hear him out." The gargoyles and his fellow Dreamvillians look at him with a mix of intrigue and hope in their eyes. Simon says, "If you help us expose Miss DreamNot and the ex dream squad chief for the frauds they are and find the real chief of police, they'll have no choice but to tell us where your friends are." Martua asks, "How are we going to do that?" Simon says, "Well we need a plan to get Miss DreamNot and the ex dream squad chief here and to get them to lead us to the real police chief." Gargantua says, "If we make a plan and we go along with you, you will then retrieve what we need?" Simon says, "Absolutely Gargantua." They remain silent for awhile as they all sit down in a circle for their negotiations. Almont says, "It's fifty-five minutes before daylight hours." Simon says, "Thanks Almont for the reminder. Oh Diana, do you want to give them some sun block to lather on their exposed skin." Rino grabs the bottle from his back pack and pulls out the bottle. He passes it to Dee, who passes it to Almont, who passes it to Jilla, who passes it to Miss LossDream, who passes it to King DreamRoyal. King DreamRoyal takes his black, oversized coat off and lathers the lotion on his hands. Simon looks at the detailing of the gargoyles necks and he sees that each one has an indentation where something can be inserted. Simon looks at the gems on his king's necklace around his neck. Simon who normally chooses to simply play the piano or any other instrument startles everyone when he starts to sing. He sings the lyrics over and over while he takes the necklace of gems off of King Régimand DreamRoyal the tenth's neck and studies their size. To his fellow Dreamvillians, it's like Simon's in a trance.

Remember truth dreamer,
They mean no harm.
They just want to be saved too.
Truth dreamer, truth dreamer
Dreamville's secret residents
Need you.
Bring them their daylight gems.
Bring them their daylight gems.
Bring them their daylight gems.
Bring them their daylight gems.
Bring them their daylight gems.
Bring them their daylight gems.

Jilla screams, "Simon, snap out of it." Simon shakes his head and looks at Jilla and then at Diana. He looks at his hands and sees he's holding his king's necklace. Almont says, "Simon, you just robbed our king." King

DreamRoyal says, "It's okay, clearly he had no idea what he was doing." Simon says, "What was I saying? Someone tell me what I was saying." He looks at all of them for an answer when Diana says, "You were singing Simon. Beautifully, I might add. The lyrics I most remember are; bring them their daylight gems." Jilla says, "Yes, you repeated these words over and over again." Simon walks up to Gargantua and he says, "Gargantua lean towards me please, Gargantua obliges and leans towards Simon. Simon runs his fingers in the indentation on this wonderful creature's neck and then he pops out a gem from the necklace. Jilla asks, "Simon what are you doing?" Simon takes the gem and places it in the indentation in Gargantua's neck. It's a perfect fit. Simon says, "Quickly everyone take a blue gem and put them in the indentations in their necks." They all grab blue gems to place them in their necks. Jilla asks, "I get it, daylight gems, you gargoyles are going to be able to live during the day with these gems." Simon says, "Precisely and they'll help us get rid of Miss DreamNot and the ex dream squad chief once we rescue their friends the chimeras." Everyone smiles at Simon, including the gargoyles. Simon says, "Quickly now the sun's beginning to rise." Diana says, "Ah... Simon..." Simon turns around to see that Almont, Jilla, Dee, Miss LossDream and King DreamRoyal have been turned into stone but the remaining four gargoyles have not yet been turned to stone. He quickly gets the blue gems in their necks. The sun's fully up and daylight breaks. The gargoyles look at the sun, the light, all around them and begin to touch themselves with disbelief. Lionessa says, "We're still alive, moving around, breathing..." Snakerina says, "Even though it's daylight hours." They, the gargoyles rejoice but soon see Simon's friends are rock statues. Gargantua puts his hand on Simon's right shoulder and says, "I'm sorry Simon. It looks like our quest will have to be postponed until tonight." They all grow quiet again as they hear the faint sound of motorized, gasoline powered vehicles start their daily commutes with their human drivers. Simon looks at Rino and he says, "Rino take out the jar of silvery grey dust." Rino picks up his back pack and takes out the jar of silvery grey dust and hands it to Simon. Simon opens the jar and as he's about to sprinkle the foreign dust all over his statuesque friends Rino says, 'Stop, you don't know what that dust does." Simon replies, "Remember the ghost of King DreamRoyal the third." Rino says, "Yes, of course I do." Simon says, "I know what this dust does." Simon sprinkles it all over them but nothing happens. Rino says, "See, you wasted it." Diana says, "I don't think he wasted it at all." Justin says, "Look." They watch the rock crumble, loosen and fall to the ground revealing their living, breathing friends. Jilla's free of the curse and hugs Simon. Almont and Miss LossDream are freed the next, followed by Dee and King DreamRoyal the tenth. They all cheer, "We're free, curse free." The gargoyles dance and laugh and bask in the sunlight. They do this for about half an hour until they notice humans driving by in their gasoline powered cars. Simon says, "We better hide out of sight of the humans or they'll kill us for sure." Gargantua says, "They'll kill us but they wouldn't kill you." Diana says, "Yes they would, they would just for being seen associating and socializing with you." Gargantua says, 'These humans have not changed over the centuries then have they?" Justin replies, "No they have, there's a little more religious tolerance, acceptance, and peace but you guys would just be completely incomprehensible for them and what they don't understand automatically triggers their fear." Diana says, "And, when they fear something or someone they tend to want to either control or destroy it." Simon says, "Quickly in the mansion." All fourteen gargoyles and all seven Dreamvillians and the two Outsiders run into the mansion. Simon closes the door behind them. Simon says, "The locks are broken." Lionessa says, "Yes, Miss DreamNot broke them one day trying to get in here to make sure that Gargantua, your friends and I were statues." Simon says, "King DreamRoyal I've been meaning to ask you, do you know why you were wearing this necklace of gems?" King DreamRoyal replies, "I have no idea." Wartua says, "We've got a problem." Jilla looks out the window too and says, "Miss DreamNot and the ex squad chief are here." Simon says, "Actually this is perfect. Gargoyles you all hide. The rest of us, we're going to make it difficult for them to catch us but we'll let them and have them bring us to the chimeras. You gargoyles will remain as inconspicuous as you possibly can and follow us." The gargoyles all hide, despite their sizes they hide successfully upstairs and downstairs. Gargantua hides behind a large, tall bookcase in the living room just off of the foyer so he can hear when he needs to signal to his fellow gargoyles to commence the chase. Jilla says, "Here they come up the steps." Simon says, "We wait right here. Diana and Justin you guys should hide and follow along with the gargoyles." Diana and Justin hide in a closet just off of the foyer. Jilla backs up from the front door and she, Almont, Rino, Dee, Miss LossDream, King DreamRoyal and Simon wait in a semi circle for the door to open.

They wait for what seems like an eternity for the two cruel Dreamvillians to enter the mansion. Finally, the door opens and the ex dream squad chief stands in the doorway speechless while he looks at the semi circle of confrontational kids, teacher and king. They hear Miss DreamNot coming closer to the front entrance of the mansion as she says, "Look at this, some dumb clog just left a necklace with gems in it out here on the ground. Ha. It's mine now." She looks at the ex dream squad chief and screams, "What's your hold up get in there." He looks back at her as her patience grows thin. She pushes him aside and sees the semi circle confrontation. Miss DreamNot says, "Oh I see, you've all escaped the gargoyles." She looks at them, trying to intimidate them and she says, "Well, you won't get away from me that easy." She pulls out her hand gun and points it at them. The ex dream squad chief pulls out his hand gun as well and points it at them. Miss DreamNot approaches King DreamRoyal and looks him in the eyes. She says, "You'll regret choosing Miss LossDream over me. I'll make you all regret banishing me, taking away what's rightfully mine." Simon says, "King DreamRoyal is a living, breathing Dreamvillian who is not an object that belongs to anyone, certainly, not to you." Miss DreamNot quickly approaches Simon and holds her gun to the temple of his head, she clicks the trigger, ready to shoot, she says, "I should shoot you right here, right now Simon Dreamlee." Jilla says, "What good would that do Miss DreamNot?" Miss DreamNot removes the gun from Simon's temple and says, "Right now, not much but later when I kill all of you including those oafs for gargoyles' friends, I'll be quite satisfied." Simon says, "You won't get what you want by killing us." Miss DreamNot says, "Oh and what do you know about what I want? I'll tell you what I want. I want all of you dead except my love, my only, King DreamRoyal. You see, if I can't have him in Dreamville, I'll have him here in the Outsiders world." Miss DreamNot says, "Come on get into the police car, come on, move along now. Any sudden moves and the ex dream squad chief here and I will shoot first to kill without asking any questions at all. Ha-ha. Ha-ha. Ha-ha." They follow Simon's lead and follow him to the police car. Jilla whispers, "I hope this works Simon." Miss DreamNot smacks Jilla on the head. Jilla says, "Owe." Miss DreamNot says, "No talking, no chatting, no ranting and especially no whispers while in my custody." Almont reacts only to get the ex dream squad chief's gun pointed to his temple as he says, "Just try me Almont Alldream." Almont says, "Okay, I surrender, you'll get no problems from me." Miss DreamNot opens the back door of the police car and says, "That's a great attitude. Now, get in the car everyone." They all get into the car, seven, Dreamvillians, Dee sits on Rino, Jilla sits on Almont, Miss LossDream Sits on King DreamRoyal and Simon gets squished against the side window. Miss DreamNot closes the car door and laughs some more, "Ha-ha. Ha-ha. Ha-ha." The dream squad chief gets in the car on the passenger side and Miss DreamNot gets in the car on the driver's side. Simon looks out the window at the mansion. Miss DreamNot starts the car and starts backing away from the mansion, turns around and drives down the quarter mile long driveway. This time she turns right and drives out of the city of Newsprings.

Simon dares to asks, "Where are you taking us Miss DreamNot?" Miss DreamNot says, "How dare you speak. You've been arrested and you dare talk to me." Simon says, "Technically we're not arrested Miss DreamNot, we're your captives. You're the mastermind kidnapper." Miss DreamNot smiles and says, "Now, Simon it's too late for you to butter me up with flattery but it's nice of you to finally realize who the real brains out of all of us really is." Simon rolls his eyes, looks in the sky and sees Gargantua flying overhead of them in plain view. Simon says, "Oh I do, I really do realize how smart you are." Almont says, "Simon… really…" Simon looks at Almont as if to tell him to shut up without actually verbalizing his thought. Almont seemingly immediately understands Simon's facial expression and nods his head. They sit quietly in the back of the police car while they watch the scenery pass by during the drive. Jilla dares to ask Simon's question again, "Where are you taking us?" Miss DreamNot says, "Jilla MusiDream, you dare to speak too do you." Jilla replies, "I do, I absolutely do dare to speak. We might be your prisoners' but we still have the right to know where we're going." The ex dream squad chief says, "Come on babe, they might as well know where their final resting place will be." Miss DreamNot screams, "WHAT HAVE I TOLD YOU ABOUT CALLING ME THAT? Don't ever call me that ever. I'm not your babe." Everyone in the car grows silent once again as Miss DreamNot's mood grows more and more intensely vicious. Dee's clearly terrified by the whole ordeal and is being held tightly by Rino who's desperately trying to keep her from freaking out but it doesn't work. Dee screams, "Let me out… Let me out, you have to let me out you terrible ugly woman. I've never done anything to you." Miss DreamNot laughs at the terror in Dee's eyes and says, "Ha-ha. Ha-ha. Ha-ha. Oh is the Rino DreamScifi's new girlfriend scared of her fate. Ha-ha. Ha-ha. That's what you get for dating a boy who crosses me, you stupid girl." Jilla laughs silently at Miss DreamNot's comments but is not immune to her sharp, evil, hurtful tongue. Miss DreamNot says, "Is that Jilla MusiDream delighting in my comments about Dee? Oh it is. Well Jilla your no better yourself being a girl who crossed me, you may not be stupid but you're no pretty catch for any boy. Wouldn't you agree Rino? After all, Jilla, he did dump you for prettier little Dee." Jilla says, "Why how dare you?" Rino says, "Hey it wasn't anything like that at all." Dee says, "What Jilla? Say what you want to say." Simon screams, "SHUT UP, ALL OF YOU. DON'T YOU SEE WHAT SHE'S DOING? SHE TRYING TO PIT US AGAINST EACH OTHER FOR HER BENEFIT. NOTHING SHE'S SAYING IS TRUE." Miss DreamNot looks in the rearview mirror at Jilla and vindictive laughter fills her eyes, "Ha-ha. HA-HA. Ha-ha." Jilla says, "Oh un-dreamy dreams, nightmares of nightmares, I want to wake up soon. Simon's right." Dee says, "You're an evil, evil, terrible, terrible, woman." Miss DreamNot just laughs and laughs. Each time she laughs her voice cackles more and more, "Ha-ha. Ha-ha. Ha-ha. Ha-ha. Ha-ha." The sound is shear torture to the Dreamvillians ears. Simon could see that her laugh even tortures the ex dream squad chief. Trying to ignore the cackle of their kidnapper, and former dream stealer, Simon looks up to the sky again and is comforted with the sight of Gargantua, Sartua, Martua, Lionessa, Snakerina, Wartua, and Wolverina as they follow the driving police car. Simon whispers, "I just wish I knew where we're going." Suddenly, Miss DreamNot turns left and drives into a tunnel with rounded cement walls. She stops the car, parks, and turns the engine off. She steps out of the police vehicle and then the ex dream squad chief steps out of the passengers side of the car as well. They close their doors and don't speak. Simon listens for them to say something, anything to indicate where they've taking them. King DreamRoyal says, "I can't let her do this. I'm going to tell her to keep me and let you all go free. Dreamville will survive without me but Dreamville needs you kids to dream and make dreams come true." Simon says, "No we're in this together and we'll get out of this together." King DreamRoyal says, "I can't allow it. I'm for the moment using my status as king to order you all to leave as soon as she lets you all go once I tell her to keep me and only me." Miss LossDream exclaims, "No, no you can't. No I can't lose you again." Jilla, Dee and Miss LossDream begin to shed tears due to all the unhappiness engulfing them at this very moment. Simon says, "Girls..." That's all he gets to say when the door he's squished against opens and he falls out of the car onto the hard ground. Jilla and Almont fall on top of Simon, squishing him against the hard ground and knocking him unconscious.

Chapter Ten – The Chimeras

The same Friday afternoon, after the three hours of driving and after being knocked unconscious, Simon finally begins to regain consciousness but his visions a bit blurry. He holds his head up and says, "Ah… my eye sight's not fully recovered yet." He wakes up to find himself on the ground and being stared at by a strange creature with a lion's body, and a birds head, wings and the tail of a lion. As he slowly regains his eyesight, he realizes that he and his friends are surrounded by exotic, intriguing and strange creatures of bizarre and normally un-natural combinations of animal parts. He takes off his sunglasses. Simon says, "You're magnificent, beautiful creatures. Diana's ancestor didn't do you justice." Jilla asks, "Simon, why are you talking to them? They can't talk." Simon looks at the half lion, half bird and says, "I think they can speak." The half lion, half bird opens his mouth and shockingly says, "We can all talk. Simon's right." Jilla asks, "Why then did you not speak all this time?" The half lion, half bird says, "None of you asked us to talk or even tried to talk to us except for Simon." Simon says, "You know my name." The half lion, half bird replies, "We all know your name little truth dreamer." Simon asks, "May I know yours?" The half lion, half bird says, "I'm a griffon and my name's Lima." The half horse, half man says, "We're centaurs and my name's Megataur and this here half horse, half human woman's Meesha." Simon says, "Nice to meet you all. What are the rest of your names?" The other half lion, half bird says with a female voice, "Hi Simon, I'm Lynelle." Jilla, Almont, Rino, Dee, and a teary eyed Miss LossDream all approach the glorious creatures as they shed their shyness and emerge from the shadows. Simon's smile fades as he says, "There's so few, so few of you." Lima says, "Yes, we're a great many less than we used to be. Many have been killed but many don't live in this part of the world." Simon says, "But only four of you. Where's the half fish, half humans?" Lima says, "The mermaids, they're still alive, but they can't leave water so they live in the rivers and streams traveling through the underground water ways. They avoid the open oceans these days." Simon notices Miss LossDream's tear stained face and looks around for king DreamRoyal. Simon says, "He didn't? Where's King DreamRoyal?" Jilla says, "He offered himself to Miss DreamNot in exchange for our freedom but she double crossed him." Almont says, "We're still her prisoners and she's taken King DreamRoyal to another undisclosed location." Rino says, "No one knows where she took him, not even the dream squad chief who she left behind to guard us." Simon looks out the cement tunnel and sees the dream squad chief snoozing on a large flat faced rock. Simon says, "He's asleep, we can just walk out of here." Simon and the Dreamvillians walk towards the entrance but Lima steps between them and the entrance and he says, "I'm afraid it's not that simple. We can't let you leave without what Miss DreamNot promised us." Jilla says, "I knew it. You creatures are on her side." Simon says, "Jilla don't jump to conclusions. They're not willingly on her side. She has leverage on them that forces them to do her bidding." Lima says, "Simon, you're quite clever." Megataur says, "Indeed, you are a clever boy and this is why we have to be careful not to let you escape." Jilla asks, "What's that sound?" They look in the direction of the exit from the cement tunnel and for the first time in their Dreamvillian lives they see, hear and smell fresh rain as it falls outside of the tunnel. Jilla runs to the opening and sticks her hand outside to catch some drops. Simon yells, "Jilla don't. We don't know what effects the rain has on our skin." Jilla pulls her hand back inside and says, "Nothing, I feel nothing. It's fine Simon." They all put their hands out to feel the sensation of rain in the palms of their hands. The ex dream squad chief wakes up, soaking wet and runs inside the cement tunnel with his gun pointed at all of them. He says, "Get back inside. I'm not going to be letting any of you escape." Rino says, "You're pathetic." The ex dream squad chief asks, "What was that?" Simon knowing that Rino just wants to distract the ex dream squad chief plays along and says, "He's right, you're pathetic. You're here instead of fighting for the woman you love." The ex dream squad chief sits on a rock located inside the cement tunnel, puts his head in his hands and mumbles, "It's no use." Simon says, "What was that?" The ex dream squad chief lifts his head and screams, "IT IS NO USE…. She'll never love me again. I'm the reason she won't open her heart to me." Jilla says, "I don't think it's that ex dream squad chief." Miss LossDream says, "She's just blinded by the evil that still lurks in her heart." Simon says, "You have to fight for her ex dream squad chief." The ex dream squad chief says, "Yes for her." They wait in silence, listening to the pitter, patter of the rain pouring out of the cloudy, grey sky. Jilla steps out into the rain and puts her hands up in the air and says, "Glorious this rain. Refreshing and look how green this rain makes the leaves on the trees." Almont runs out and does the same as Jilla. The ex dream squad chief says, "Get back in here, please get back in here before, they..." Simon says, "They what?" The bushes start shaking and growling as a large male cougar jumps out of the bushes and pins Jilla to the ground. His mouth snarls revealing his large, sharp white teeth. Another three cougars jump out of the bushes and surround Almont. Rino says, "Oh my un-dreamy dreams." Simon says, "Quick ex dream squad chief get your gun out and shoot it in the air." The ex dream squad chief runs out along with Rino and Simon, he points his gun in the air and attempts to shoot it but it's jammed. The ex dream squad chief says, "My gun... it's jammed. I can't get it to shoot." Almont starts to fling his arms frantically to scare the cougars but it doesn't deter them. Rino runs and jumps on the back of the cougar that's pinned Jilla to the ground and begins to hold on to the fierce animal's neck as if it were a horse, he holds on for dear life because now if he falls off he will be their next meal. The male cougar jumps towards the bushes and off of Jilla. Simon runs to Jilla and helps her up. Simon says, "Jilla get in the tunnel." Jilla freezes in her spot." Simon yells, "Jilla, get back in the tunnel." Jilla runs into the tunnel and watches with Miss LossDream and the chimeras. Meanwhile, Rino's flung around by the huge male cougar while Almont has managed to confuse the three cougars attempts to pounce on him. Jilla screams, "Almont look out." Almont hears her on time to bob as one of the cougars pounce over his head and onto the cougar across from him sending both cougars tumbling into the bushes. As the night begins as the sun goes down, Almont now faces one cougar. However, not for long as the other two emerge from the bushes. Still on top of the original cougar, Rino gets flung into the cement tunnel by the male cougar. Dee runs to Rino and hugs him. Rino says, "I'm alright Dee." The wind picks up and the rain whips Simon and the ex dream squad chief in the face as they approach Almont to pull him inside the tunnel but instead all three of them are surrounded by the four cougars. The ex dream squad chief points his gun in the air to attempt to shoot again but a cougar lunges at him causing him to drop his gun. It's now dark out and the male griffon flies out of the cement tunnel and lands in front of the largest male cougar. Lima says, "Leave now and find another meal." The cougars surround Lima, snarling, growling, and bearing their sharp teeth and long, sharp claws. Lima yells, "Simon, you and your friend run in the tunnel." They run in the tunnel and watch the griffon and the cougars with everyone else. Jilla asks Lynelle, "Why did it take him so long to go out there?" Simon replies for Lynelle and says, "Because Jilla, they, like the gargoyles, cannot live in the sunlight without their daylight gems." Lynelle says, "That's right. And, Miss DreamNot has them. That's the leverage she has over us." Lima yells, "Leave now cougars." He quickly flies up into the air as the four cougars pounce. They crash into each other knocking the breath out of them. They tumble to the ground landing on their four paws but are visibly shaken but not convinced to leave. Lynelle runs out and says, "Leave now cougars. They're not your supper and neither are we." Simon remarks, "They're not leaving." The cougars seem to be even more angry and determined now than they were when they first arrived. The cougars pounce on Lima and Lynelle pounces on the cougars. The centaurs run out and kick the cougars with their hind legs as hard as they can, striking them in their faces. Simon says, "They're only angering those cougars." There's blood flying through the air from all of their wounds.

Suddenly, they hear a loud screech from the cloudy night sky. Simon looks up but the rains still pouring and his eyes are pounded with rain drops affecting his vision. He listens intently as the fight between the chimeras and the earthly cougars' continues. Jilla says, "Simon they're going to get killed by those cougars." Simon says, "You're right we have to help them." Simon runs out of the tunnel along with everyone else following behind him and he stops. Simon looks around and sees rocks peeking out from the grass that's been flattened by the pouring rain. Simon says, "Grab rocks and start throwing them at the cougars." Almont says, "Careful not to hit the chimeras." Everyone picks up the rocks and start pelting the cougars as hard as they can." Jilla screams, "It's no use they're killing them." That screech from out of the night sky suddenly brings the cougars to a frozen halt as they too stare into the night sky. Simon hears Gargantua say, "They're down there. Is everyone, alright down there?" Gargantua, Wartua, Martua, Sartua, Wolverina, Snakerina, Lionessa, swoop down and grab the cougars by their tails and start spinning them in the air. Gargantua lets go of one of the cougars and it flies through the air to the far end of the Outsiders forest. Wartua, Martua and Sartua release the cougars they have in their hands and they also fly through the air in the direction of their cougar leader. Simon says, "Gargantua, thank you." Gargantua replies to Simon, "Simon sorry we didn't get here faster but we lost your trail when we had to hide from and airplane." Sartua says, "Yeah if the human pilot would have seen us it would have been chaotic." Lionessa says, "Gargantua, they're all injured badly. We need to get them some help." The gargoyles walk up to the griffons and the centaurs and look at their wounds, wounds inflicted by the hungry cougars. Jilla says, "Quickly everyone, rip a part of your clothes to wrap around their wounds and stop the bleeding." Rino says, "She's right, follow me I'll show you how." Everyone rips pieces off of their clothing and follows Rino's instructions. Rino says, "Wrap around, directly on top of the wounds to stop the bleeding and tie the dressing in a tight knot but leave enough loose tension for the wound to breathe." A half hour later, the griffons and the centaurs can walk but are a little weak. With this crisis temporarily averted, Simon asks, "Where are Diana and Justin?" Gargantua replies, "We elected not to bring them with us that way if we're caught by the humans who fear us, they will not be associated with us and ridiculed or worse murdered." The dream squad chief says, "Where did you leave them?" Gargantua looks perplexed at the sight of the ex dream squad chief. Simon says, "Miss DreamNot turned her back on him and has now taken King DreamRoyal the tenth to another location. We don't know where." Gargantua says, "Diana and Justin are at the mansion. They should be safe there." The dream squad chief says, "Oh no… That's where she was taking King DreamRoyal." Jilla says, "How do you know, she just left without telling us or you anything." The dream squad chief says, "I know, I just know." Simon says, "We have to get to the mansion before she harms Diana and Justin." Lima weakly says, "Gargantua, you have your life back." Gargantua turns to Lima and says, "Yes, indeed, Simon got them back for us." Simon says, "Well not really, King DreamRoyal was wearing them and I just remembered the lyrics from my dream." Almont says, "It doesn't matter, we need to find King DreamRoyal and get back to Dreamville." Simon says, "Gargantua can you fly us all including the Chimeras back to the MagicDream's mansion?" Lima interjects and says, "Ah… that won't be necessary for me, I can fly myself." Lynelle, Megataur and Meesha simultaneously say, "We can too." Gargantua turns to Simon and says, "In that case, we gargoyles are more than happy to help out you and your fellow Dreamvillians." Simon says, "That's great, absolutely. We have to get going now. Time is imperative."

Gargantua picks up Simon. Wartua picks up Almont. Sartua picks up the ex dream squad chief. Wolverina picks up Jilla. Lionessa picks up Miss LossDream. Martua picks up Rino and Snakerina picks up Dee. They all fly up into the night sky with the rest of the gargoyles and the chimeras follow closely behind. Gargantua says, "Not to fast so our chimera friends can keep up." All of a sudden, Lima flies up besides Gargantua and challenges him to a flying race. Lima says, "Don't fly slowly because we'll beat you there." Gargantua playfully laughs and says, "Ha-ha. Ha-ha. Alright, it's a race." The gargoyles pick up their pace and fly quickly and swiftly through the air as do the chimeras that seem to have recovered from their brawl with the cougars. Simon laughs, "Ha-ha. This is fun!" Jilla says, "So fun!"

Almont says, "Oh my dreams please don't drop me." Wartua laughs and says to Almont, "Ha-ha. Just don't look down." Almont hadn't yet looked down but now he does and he covers his eyes. Rino says, "Faster, can we go faster." The gargoyles and the chimeras oblige and fly even faster through the wind and rain through the night until they reach the mansion. Dee screams in fear so Snakerina covers her mouth with her hand and says with a slight slither, "Stop girl, it's not that scary." Dee calms herself down and Snakerina takes her hand off of her mouth. Dee looks down at the earth and faints. Snakerina holds onto Dee and laughs, "Ha-ha."

They fly in a circle above the front yard and Simon says, "Look there's Miss DreamNot's police car. She's here Gargantua." Gargantua says, "Gargoyles, friends fly downward." They fly towards the front yard and land softly on the ground. Simon sees the front doors are already open and without hesitation runs inside the mansion. Almont and Jilla follow closely behind him. When it dawns on the others what's happening, they too run inside the house. The gargoyles and the chimeras follow behind Simon and his fellow Dreamvillians. Simon stops and everyone behind him stops. He looks around the foyer but sees nothing, he says, "There in the basement." Simon runs downstairs to the basement but discovers nothing in the room where he originally found his Dreamvillians friends. He runs upstairs into the kitchen but nothing. He runs to the dining room, the living room and the study but still nothing. He runs upstairs and opens every door in the upstairs of the house but there's no sign of Diana, Justin, King DreamRoyal or the evil Miss DreamNot. He looks back at everyone. He says, "They're not here. If they were here, they're definitely gone. She's taken them somewhere else." He looks around for clues, anything that could lead them to their new location. Miss LossDream begins to cry again and says, "Oh my un-dreamy nightmares, I'm sorry kids, I just didn't think there'd be any more problems and I'd be married by this time tomorrow and now it seems I'll never be married." Simon says, "You'll be married Miss LossDream, please stop crying for now and be strong." Jilla says, "Look Simon on that chair in the corner of that room," Simon looks into a room with red walls and large windows. There's a fireplace against the far wall and a chair in the corner, on the chair is the black oversized coat that King DreamRoyal the tenth was wearing. Simon says, "They were here." Simon sees another indication they were there in that room because besides the King's black, oversized coat is Diana's ring that she wore on her right hand. Simon says, "That's Diana's ring with the garnet stone. I noticed her ring when I got to know her once Rino and I accepted that Justin and she weren't trying to hurt us but help us." Simon gets a strong feeling flush over him which makes him dizzy, just as he's about to fall over onto the floor, Jilla runs and catches him. Almont runs behind Jilla to provide more support. Simon comes to consciousness and says, "They're here. There's another chamber in this mansion that we haven't discovered and I haven't even ever dreamed about it either." Jilla asks, "How can you be sure?" Simon says, "I just feel a connection." Rino says, "A connection. You mean you feel Diana's presence is close." Simon says, "Yes." Almont and Jilla look at each other, Jilla turns to Simon and she says, "Simon, lead us to them." Simon regains his strength and stands on his own two feet. He looks around the room and says, "This room has a secret. We have to discover the secret." Rino steps back and grabs Dee's hand. Dee holds his hand. Jilla sees this but ignores this gesture focusing her attention on Simon and their quest to find his outsider friends and King DreamRoyal the tenth. Almont sees Jilla's reaction and he steps into her view of the new lovebirds and smiles at her, Jilla smiles back at Almont.

Simon tunes out everyone around him as he strives to find what he's looking for even though he's not a hundred percent sure what that might be. He simply feels what he needs to find is in the very room they're standing in. Simon scopes out the room, examining every detail, inch by inch. Jilla asks, "Simon what are you doing?" Simon hushes her, "Shush." A couple minutes later Simon says, "I need everyone to leave this room right now. Please wait in the hallway." All the gargoyles, chimeras and Dreamvillians leave the room to let Simon investigate his hunch. He looks around the room starting with the fireplace. He taps the fireplace placing his ear against the rock to try and hear if it's hollow. He walks along the walls doing the same process but finds nothing. He sits in the chair and looks out the open door. Almont looks inside the room from the hallway, he sees Simon sitting there, and Almont grabs Jilla's hand and pulls her inside the room with him and they walk towards Simon. The gargoyles follow Almont and Jilla as well as the chimeras and then all the Dreamvillians. They all stare at Simon, waiting for his next move. Simon looks up and says, "I'm stumped." He looks at them and begins to laugh hysterically, "Ha-ha. I'm stumped. Ha-ha." He laughs so much he falls over in the chair. With the chair fallen over, King DreamRoyal's black coat is no longer hiding a trap door. Simon sees the trap door and quickly regains his composure. Simons says, "A trap door." Almont says, "I see it, another trap door." Almont walks to the trap door while Jilla helps Simon up to his feet for the second time. Almont looks at Simon while he opens the trap door. Simon says, "What do you see." Before Almont can answer, Simon hears Diana's voice say, "Simon is that you?" Simon runs to the trap door and says, "Yes Diana, it's me." Diana starts to cry and says, "Simon go back to Dreamville. Miss DreamNot has what she wants you don't have to bother yourself with us anymore." King DreamRoyal says, "She's right. Go home Simon and tell Miss LossDream, I'm sorry." Miss LossDream runs to look down the trap door and she genuinely sincerely says, "No, we're not leaving you." Simon says, "Diana, I'm not leaving you down there." Simon starts climbing down the ladder into the secret dungeon like room. Almont follows close behind him and so does Jilla and Miss LossDream. Jilla looks around and asks, "What is this place?" Simon starts untying Diana's hands. Almont unties Justin's hands while Miss LossDream unties the King's hands. Diana says, "We have no idea what's the purpose of this room." Justin says, "We didn't even know it existed." Simon says, "We better get out of here." They climb back up the ladder and into the room." Miss LossDream and King DreamRoyal hug each other. Diana hugs Simon and everyone's happy for a very brief second.

They hear a commotion outside of the mansion. Gargantua looks out the window and says, "It's happening again." Simon runs to the window and sees an Outsider mob with a container that indicates the word gasoline and he says, "A mob with gasoline containers and…" Diana looks out the window and says, "They have barbecue lighters." Justin says, "They want to burn this mansion to the ground." They watch as they spread the gasoline all over the front of the house and all over the shed. Simon asks, "Where's Miss DreamNot? She couldn't have known they were planning this ambush or else she wouldn't have brought you here. She wouldn't kill King DreamRoyal." Jilla says, "You're right. She's still delusional about their relationship, thinking he can still fall in love with her." Almont says, "Listen they're chanting something." Through the singing they hear a male voice yell, "We saw you, you devils. We know you're in there and we're not afraid." They sing loudly. Gargantua says to Simon, "It's happening again, history's repeating itself in this modern age." Jilla remarks, "Those lyrics are terribly untrue." Simon says, "Yes but they don't realize that and they don't want to learn the truth either." Jilla says, "But why?" Diana puts her hand on Jilla's shoulder and says, "It's just their way. Don't be mad at them just try and understand where they're misguided beliefs stem from." The lyrics are haunting the gargoyles that visibly quiver at the memory. The chimeras are also visibly scared by the song promoting death to the gargoyles like misguided propaganda. Simon says, "Poor, misguided souls." Justin says, "It's propaganda of the worse kind."

Lions, symbols the deadly sin of pride
Lions no more we fear thee.
We will burn you and your witchcraft worshipers.
Burn, burn, burn and be gone.

Dogs can't resist the sin of temptation.
Dogs are always hungry, stealing food.
Dogs are sinners, thieves.
Burn, burn, burn and be gone.

Wolf, the devil's pet you are and we know.
Wolf, you are the deadly sin of greed.
Wolves are sinners and the pet of evil.
Burn, burn, burn and be gone.

Snake slithers, slides, and hides.
Snake is a sinner.
Snake symbolizes the deadly sin of envy.
Burn, burn, burn and be gone.

Goat, so cleverly disguised as cute.
Goats are the most evil sinner.
Goats represent the deadliest sin of lust.
Burn, burn, burn and be gone.

Monkey, stupid and ugly monkey,
They are nature gone awry to punish humans for their sins.
Monkeys are the living deadly sin of sloth.
Burn, burn, burn and be gone.

Burn, burn, burn and be gone.
Burn, burn, burn and be gone.
Burn, burn, burn and be gone.
Burn, burn, burn and be gone.

Chapter Eleven – Quashing Miss Dreamnot

Diana, Goes in the hallway and picks up the phone. Simon follows her out into the hallway and asks, "What are you doing?" Diana says, "The only thing I can think of which is to call the fire department so they can come and stop the fire when they start burning down my home." She puts the phone to her ear and says, "The lines dead." Justin comes into the hallway and says, "Diana did you call someone?" Diana replies, "I tried calling the fire department but the phone lines dead. Try your cell phone." Justin checks his pockets and says, "I don't have it." Simon says, "Here Diana. This is a virtual communicator. I want you to hang onto it in case we get separated. If we do, I'll use my friend Almont's to contact you." Diana nods her head in agreement. She says, "Okay." They can hear the mob outside getting louder and larger. In the distance they hear the sound of sirens pulling into the front yard. Simon, Diana, Justin, Almont and Jilla run to the window and look out into the front yard. Simon says, "Those red trucks must be fire trucks." Diana says, "They are." Jilla says, "Look more police officers." Simon says, "Where's Miss DreamNot? I'm sure she hasn't just disappeared and left King DreamRoyal. Something's not right." Almont says, "There she is with the rest of the human police officers." Simon says, "She's saying something. She's ordering them to burn the mansion to the ground." Miss DreamNot yells, "Burn it, burn this ugly, evil monstrosity to the ground. Burn it to the ground." Diana says, "Oh my... what are we going to do? What can we do? We have to do something to stop them. There's too much history here for it to go up in flames." Simon turns to everyone and says, "Everybody, we have to stay together as a group and run outside. Once we run outside we have to make them chase us so they get distracted from the idea of burning down this historical mansion of the family of MagicDream's." Gargantua says, "Agreed. We'll fly into the sky low enough that they can see us and chase us but high enough they can't harm us." Gargantua picks up Simon. Wartua picks up Almont.

Wolverina picks up Jilla. Lionessa picks up Miss LossDream. Martua picks up Rino. Snakerina picks up Dee. Dartua picks up King DreamRoyal the tenth. Dogerina picks up Diana. Larantua picks up Justin. Sartua goes to picks up the ex dream squad chief who's running downstairs to the foyer and runs outside. Sartua says, "I think the ex dream squad chief has flipped sides again." Simon looks outside and sees the ex dream squad chief run up to Miss DreamNot, points at the window of the room where they're all located. Simon says, "Gargantua we've got to fly now." Gargantua says, "You heard the truth dreamer, we've got to go now." They all start to fly out of the room following Gargantua and Simon. Simon looks up at Gargantua and says, "As soon as you fly out the front door, go straight up into the sky or they'll pull guns out and shoot us." Gargantua says, "Hopefully they haven't already started shooting." Gargantua approaches the front door at a very high speed, out and up into the sky. Simon looks down and sees the ex dream squad chief driving off in the police car and Miss DreamNot chasing him. The rest of the gargoyles successfully make it out of the mansion, even though, Larantua and Justin were both skimmed by two bullets but not severely hurt. Gargantua yells, "Larantua, are you both okay?" Larantua looks at Justin and asks, "Are you hurt?" Justin looks up at Larantua and replies, "No, I'm not hurt." Larantua yells back to Gargantua through the noise of gun shots and streaming bullets, "We're both fine Gargantua." Gargantua screams, "Higher, fly higher." The gargoyles increase their elevation slightly so the humans can still follow them. Gargantua leads the running mob down the quarter mile driveway, Simon says, "Good fly to the cemetery." Gargantua says, "Where it all began." Simon says, "Yes, Gargantua, where it all began, it's our only hope to get back to Dreamville with the chimeras this time around." Gargantua says, "Then this is where I'll fly us to." Simon says, "Fly us over streets so they can follow." Gargantua says, "Okay little truth dreamer." Simon looks down at the angry mob and says, "May their God and my dreams forgive us and them for what we feel we need to do to quash this negative behavior." Gargantua says, "The rains still coming down hard." The rain pelts Simon's face like little tiny pebbles. Simon says, "Yes it is." Wartua flies besides Gargantua and Almont says, "Simon look there's the ex dream squad chief's police car. I recognize the car number." Simon says, "Thirteen?" Almont says, "Yes and look he's heading off the mob." Simon says, "I guess he didn't flip after all. We still have to get to the cemetery." Almont says, "Ah he's picking up Miss DreamNot." Simon looks and says, "There, over there. That's the cemetery." Gargantua says, "I know but you said to lead them there." Simon says, "Ah right." Gargantua asks, "Is there a change in plan." Simon says, "No there isn't. There was no plan to begin with." Gargantua and the other gargoyles and chimeras keep flying through the sky just above the street to lead the mob to the cemetery.

Gargantua lands in the cemetery along with all the others. The gargoyles put their passengers down on the ground and they all run to Simon. Almont says, "What now Simon?" Simon says, "We wait for Miss DreamNot, she has the chimeras daylight gems." Simon looks around the cemetery and says to Gargantua, "Gargantua, do you have the golden dust?" Gargantua replies, "Yes, all my fellow gargoyles have some." Simon says, "Great, Gargantua, you and all of you are going to fly up and cover the mob of humans with the golden dust. Make sure it's just the humans but not Miss DreamNot or the ex dream squad chief." Gargantua looks at his fellow Gargoyles and says, "Everyone has their golden dust ready?" Sartua, Wartua, Larantua, Martua, Lionessa, Wolverina, Goaterina, Monkerina, Snakerina, Eaglerina, Dartua, Dogerina, and Eagantua look at Gargantua and they all reply, "Yes we have our golden dust." The gargoyles line up side by side forming a wall between the Dreamvillians and the human mob. The angry human mob comes charging into the cemetery and Gargantua says, "Alright, on my mark…" Unbearable seconds tick by as they all wait for Gargantua to give the signal to dust the humans. Diana grabs Simon's hand and they hold hands. Almont asks, "How many of them are there?" Simon says, "Many. I just hope the gargoyles have enough golden dust for all of them." Simon finishes his sentence just on time to hear Gargantua give the uniquely gargoyle signal. Gargantua screeches a piercing, paralyzing sound that stops the humans in their tracks. They hold their ears to prevent themselves from hearing Gargantua but they can't resist. The sound only affects the humans but not the Dreamvillians. The gargoyles fly up into the air, their wings creating massive amounts of wind being swept towards the people underneath them. They spread the golden dust vigorously, quickly, effectively and efficiently until all the humans are lying fast asleep on the cemetery ground beneath them. Suddenly, another mob comes and the gargoyle, Gargantua, screeches again, paralyzing this new wave of humans as well. They spread the dust and this group lies in the middle of the cement street. Simon, Almont, Rino, Jilla, Dee, Diana, Justin, Miss DreamNot and Miss LossDream cheer as the sounds of silence fill the night. The chimeras are quiet in their corner as they soak in the events of the night that's not yet over as the police car with number thirteen approaches the cemetery from the opposite direction of the mob.

Simon says, "Chimeras hide in the shadows." The gargoyles are just now returning and landing besides the Dreamvillians. Simon says, "Gargoyles hide in the shadows as best you can."

Miss DreamNot parks the police car and opens the driver's side door, she pulls out a rifle with a silencer attached to the end and begins running towards the Dreamvillians while she screams, "You haven't won yet Simon Dreamlee. You and your friends will die before I let you get back to Dreamville." Simon yells, "Miss DreamNot, we're so happy to see you." She runs up to him, stops and points the rifle at him, she says, "Don't patronize and be condescending with me shorty." Diana squeezes Simon's hand and Simon squeezes her hand back. Miss DreamNot says, "Oh ho... look who's got a girlfriend. A human and a Dreamvillian, you'll never be together." Simon says, "Technically, she's a Dreamvillian." Miss DreamNot screams, "Centuries removed. She'll never be accepted back into Dreamville, that I guarantee you." Miss DreamNot puts her hand out and lifts a strand of Diana's brunette hair and says, "It's a shame really, isn't it Simon, after all, she's the perfect height for you." She cackles like she always does when she thinks she has the upper hand in their continuous battle. Simon says, "Nice necklace Miss DreamNot." Miss DreamNot lifts her necklace with her free hand and says, "Indeed, it was a gift to me from my King and my love. Wasn't it Régimand?" King DreamRoyal the tenth replies, "Not at all. You stole it when it landed on the ground at the MagicDreams' mansion." This angered Miss DreamNot so incredibly so she takes the rifle and shoots it towards Miss LossDream and the bullet skims her hand. Miss LossDream exclaims, "Owe, ah..." Miss LossDream raises her hand to her lips to cool the burning sensation left on her hand from the kiss of the outskirts of the bullet that hits a tombstone and ricochets towards the church breaking a window. They all listen to the glass shatter and fall behind them but no one dares turn around to look at the broken window. Miss DreamNot screams, "How dare you lie to me and make me look like a fool in front of my servants." Clearly distracted Simon releases his grip on Diana's hand and approaches Miss DreamNot from the side. She turns more towards King DreamRoyal and Miss LossDream as she screams more, "I'm the one you love not her, not this temporary interlude in our love. We can work through this hard time in our relationship." Simon slowly reaches his hand out as he eyes the clasp of the necklace on the back of Miss DreamNot's neck. Just as Simon's about to get the clasp, Miss DreamNot un-expectantly quickly turns around and shoots her rifle, Simon manages to duck on time to not get the bullet in the head.

The bullet flies through the air and through the bushes. Suddenly, they hear a dog yelp in pain as its hind leg is struck by the bullet. The girls all gasp in sympathy for the dog. Rino jumps out behind Miss DreamNot and being taller easily un-clasps the necklace. She turns around to see who dared to un-clasp her prized necklace. Meanwhile, Simon catches the necklace before it hits the ground and throws it into the shadows. Miss DreamNot backs away from the line of Dreamvillians and says, "That's enough tomfoolery out of all of you." She points the gun at Rino and says, "Give me back my gift, my necklace of gems." Simon says, "Never. They're not yours. They're not even the King's." Miss DreamNot says, "Really, then who's are they?" The deep voice of Gargantua says, "The gems are ours." The chimeras and the gargoyles come out of the shadows with their shiny gems in their necks and their shiny animal eyes. They circle around Miss DreamNot and Lima says, "You were never intending to give us our gems back were you Miss DreamNot?" Gargantua says, 'No you were going to keep them all to yourself. You were going to kill us by having this mob burn the mansion down with us inside. You were even going to kill King DreamRoyal who you claim to love so much so you could keep the gems." Miss DreamNot says, "But I, I didn't know that you all were in the mansion." Wartua says, "Yes you did. You did know." Lionessa says, "We know because of the song they were singing. We heard that song in the thirteen hundreds and now again today in twenty ten." Miss DreamNot says, "No you don't understand. I can explain." Gargantua flies off to the police car where the ex-dream squad chief sits and pulls him out of the car. He flies him to Miss DreamNot and puts him on the ground in front of her. Gargantua grabs her rifle and throws it on the ground among the sleeping mob of humans. Simon says, "Listen, there's sirens coming this way." Diana says, "All this commotion must of woke up some of the people that live around here." Simon makes his way past the gargoyles and grabs Miss DreamNot's handcuffs and he cuffs her. Simon turns to the ex dream squad chief and says, "You are going to turn yourselves in as the imposters that you are. Gargantua takes the ex dream squad chief's hand cuffs and he cuffs him. Gargantua flies them back to the police car and places them on the cement street just in front of the car. Gargantua hears banging coming from the trunk and faint voices yelling, "Let us out. Let us out of here. Anybody, somebody help us." Gargantua flies back to Simon and says, "Simon there's people in the trunk of the car." Simon hears the sirens loudly and says, "We have no time to free them, the human police will do that. We have to figure out how to open the ancient passage to get back to Dreamville." Simon hands the remaining gems on the necklace back to King DreamRoyal. He puts it around Miss LossDream's neck, hugs her and says, "This is yours for safe keeping my true love."

The police cars begin to arrive and the Dreamvillians, chimeras and gargoyles hide in the shadows that are slowly disappearing as day slowly begins to break despite the clouds and the never ceasing rain. Simon and Gargantua stand in front of the graffiti filled rock wall located way at the back of the cemetery out of the sight of the human police officers that are arresting Miss DreamNot and the ex dream squad chief. They open the trunk and the real police chief and his assistant jump out of the trunk. They hear the real police chief say, "Arrest those two, they kidnapped us and took us who knows where in the middle of the woods for the past month." Miss DreamNot yells, "It's not my fault, Simon Dreamlee's the one at fault." Simon looks at Gargantua and whispers, "We better hurry." Simon looks at the drawings trying to figure out if there's some kind of indication regarding how to open the ancient passage way from the Outsiders world. Simon whispers, "We may not be able to get back home through this passage." Suddenly, Gargantua grabs Simon and shoves him behind him. Gargantua stiffens like a statue, although, he's not really and stares forward. They hear one of the human police officers say, "There's nothing back here but an ugly, old, gargoyle statue." They hear the human police chief say, "Alright, well let's get these drunken bums to the drunk-tank for the rest of the night or at least until they wake up. I'll put the call out for the police vans." Gargantua senses the humans' presence gone and is not stiff anymore. Simon whispers, "Cool trick." Gargantua whispers, "Yeah it comes in handy." Simon's eyes fall on a drawing of a gem, but a gem that's a different color from the rest. Everyone comes out of the shadows and approaches Simon and Gargantua. Simon walks towards Miss LossDream and picks up the necklace. Simon whispers, "All the gems are a whitish blue but this one's yellow. This one opens the ancient passage." He takes the yellow gem out of the necklace and looks at the rock walls surface. He sees nothing until he looks at the ground at a tiny rock that's maybe a few millimeters larger than the gem. This rock also has an indentation in it that fits the gem. Simon whispers, "I dream this is the key home." He places the yellow gem in the indentation and the rock wall becomes wavy. Simon holds his hand out and it goes through the wall. Simon whispers, "Okay Rino, lead everyone home." Rino nods his head in agreement and he whispers, "Okay everyone, follow me." The Dreamvillians, the gargoyles, the chimeras all enter into the ancient passage. Simon stays behind for a few moments to say his farewells. Diana takes Simon's hand and she whispers, "I'm honored to have met you Simon Dreamlee of Dreamville. I'll never forget you." Simon smiles at her and he whispers, "The honor was all mine; Diana. How many Dreamvillians do you or I know that can say they met a direct descendant of Master MagicDream?" Diana smiles at Simon, Justin interrupts their moment when he whispers, "It was great to meet you Simon and thanks for everything but hurry up you two or we'll get caught by the police." Diana leans in and gives Simon a kiss on the cheek. The rain stops, the sun peeks through the dispersing clouds, Simon blushes and she whispers, "Goodbye." She releases her grip, Simon turns around and just before walking into the wall he turns back to say goodbye too but Justin and Diana are already gone. Simon picks up the yellow gem and jumps into the wavy wall that instantly becomes solid rock once he's past through. He walks through the illusion of the waterfall. He places his hand on the cheek that Diana kissed. It's almost as if he can feel the warmth of her lips on his cheek.

Simon enters the room that looks more like a gigantic hole in the ground and everyone's waiting for him. King DreamRoyal the third's ghostly figure floats besides King DreamRoyal the tenth. Simon says, "I see you've met." Everyone laughs cheerfully. Jilla says, "We're home." Almont says, "We're home." Everyone says, "We're home." Simon looks at the gargoyles and the chimeras and says, "You're all home too." Gargantua and the other gargoyles start pushing a large rock over the ancient passage to the outside world recovering it now, properly, and forever. Simon feels the reality of missing someone, someone he'll probably never be able to see again. Sadness floods over him as they begin their journey through the tunnels back to DreamRoyal castle. Almont senses his friend's anguish and says, "It's for the best Simon. She's more human than Dreamvillian being so many centuries removed." Simon looks at Almont and says, "Somehow I don't care about that at all. I felt a real connection with her." Jilla startles the two who thought they were having a private conversation by saying, "A connection, like the three of us have." She smiles at both of them and Almont never being able to resist Jilla's smile, smiles back at her. Simon says, "Yeah, like the three of us thirteen year olds." Jilla squeezes her way between the two of them and puts her arms around them as they walk down the last tunnel to the laboratory. Everyone climbs up the ladder and into the DreamRoyal castle's basement. King DreamRoyal says, "Please make it to our wedding this afternoon." Jilla says, "We'll be there King DreamRoyal." Simon says, "I wouldn't miss it." Almont says, "The wedding must go on." Jilla laughs, "Ha-ha." Simon laughs and says, "Ha-ha, how cliché." Almont laughs, "Ha-ha." Rino and Dee laugh too. The gargoyles climb into the basement and Gargantua asks, "What's so funny?" The chimeras climb into the basement. King DreamRoyal walks to the secret trap door, closes it and covers it with the carpet. He says, "I would like to invite all of you to Miss LossDream and my wedding this dreamy Saturday afternoon at three at the summer festival grounds." Miss LossDream says, "I'd be honored if you all escorted me down the aisle, especially you two, Gargantua and Lionessa." Lionessa says, "We'd be honored." Gargantua says, "Are you sure you want all of Dreamville to see us? To see, that we are in fact living breathing creatures." King DreamRoyal the tenth says, "I certainly do." The ghost of King DreamRoyal the third says, "I think it's a splendid idea. I wish I had thought of that myself when Master MagicDream gave me those gems for safe keeping, of course, he didn't tell me what they were for." Simon says, "Come gargoyles, you'll be amazed at how open minded Dreamvillians really are." Jilla says, "Yeah, you're free, free to live as you please in the sanctity of Dreamville." Sartua, Wartua, Larantua, Dartua all say, "Gargantua, we should go." Gargantua says, "Well then it is definitely an honor to go to the royal wedding but it is even more of an honor to live among you great dreamers, especially you, little truth dreamer." Simon smiles at Gargantua and says, "Great, we'll see you all at three. Be ready to eat." King DreamRoyal contacts the media clowns and says, "I need you do to a virtualcast announcing that the royal dream wedding is taking place at three and that Simon Dreamlee is a real, dreamy, Dreamvillian hero. Thank you." Miss LossDream says, "Well everyone, hurry home, get cleaned up and I'll see you all again as Queen DreamRoyal." Everyone runs upstairs, out the front door and down DreamRoyal hill in separate directions to get ready for the wedding. Simon looks back at the gargoyles and chimeras that stay in the DreamRoyal Castle's yard. Jilla says, "Oh Simon, they're safe now. You don't need to worry anymore." Simon says, "I don't. Do I?" Jilla says, "Bye guys, I'll see you at the wedding." Simon and Almont wave at Jilla as they walk towards their side of Dreamville. Simon walks into his hover driveway and says to Almont, "I'll never forget her." Almont says, "I know you won't but it's forbidden Simon." Simon nods his head in agreement and Almont says, "I'll see you at the wedding." Simon says, "Yeah see you." Simon watches Almont walk in the direction of his house and he whispers, "Forbidden love in Dreamville. Oh my un-dreamy dreams but dreams are supposed to come true here. Aren't they?" Simon walks up his hover driveway and in the front door where his parents give him a hero's welcome with hugs and kisses all over his cheeks. Mr. Dreamlee says, "Welcome home son." Mrs. Dreamlee says, "We just saw the virtualcast commanded by King DreamRoyal himself. You're truly amazing Simon, my, son." Simon says, "Thanks, it was nothing really. I should get ready for the royal dream wedding." Mr. Dreamlee says, "Okay son, you do that." Mrs. Dreamlee says, "We'll wait for you to come down and we'll go to the festivities as a family." Simon says, "I'd like that. Oh and dad, I need a new virtual communicator. I seem to have lost mine." Mr. Dreamlee says, "Sure thing son, in fact, I'll go out and get you one right now before the Dreamville mall is closed and everyone in Dreamville's at the royal dream wedding." He exits by the front door and hovers off to the Dreamville mall. Simon walks upstairs into the bathroom and takes a shower. He gets out, towels off and gets dressed in his tuxedo that's already hanging on the door. He brushes his teeth, flosses and rinses his mouth. He touches his cheek once again. He still feels the warmth of Diana's lips on his cheek. Simon walks to the bathroom door and opens the door. His parents stand there in front of him and his father holds out a new virtual communicator. Simon takes it out of his hand and says, "Thanks dad and mom." Simon opens the package and voice activates and programs it to recognize only his voice. Once he does this, his parents and Simon go downstairs and out the front door. They climb into their hover car and hover to the summer festivities grounds for the royal dream wedding. His father's virtualcast streams a live virtual newscast and the media clown says, "It's a dreamy, cloudless day in Dreamville as the royal dream wedding is about to come true for Miss LossDream and King DreamRoyal the tenth on this dreamy, lovely, romantic, perfect Saturday. Three in the afternoon on Saturday approaches so tick, tock, Dreamvillians it's time to get to the festival grounds and celebrate our royal Family's dreamalicious wedding, happy and dreamy Saturday Dreamvillians."

Chapter Twelve – The Royal Dream Wedding Come True

Mr. Dreamlee hovers into the hover car parkade for the dreamy summer festival grounds. Silently, they get out of the hover car and walk into the grounds. They take their seats up front as per their assigned seating. Simon looks around at the crowd of invites and tries to see Almont and Jilla but he doesn't see them anywhere. He looks forward and then he feels a tap on his shoulder. He turns around and Almont and Jilla, holding hands, smile at him, Jilla says, "Come sit with us." Simon looks at his parents and Mrs. Dreamlee says, "Go ahead." Simon, Almont and Jilla walk to the very front and sit in the seats. Almont says, "Wow, these are great seats." Simon says, "Yeah they are." Jilla says, "The decorations are so dreamy aren't they." Almont says in typical boy style, "Yeah dreamy." King DreamRoyal comes down the aisle with Gargantua as his best man and the rest of the male gargoyles as his wedding party. The Dreamvillians gasp at the sight. Simon here's whispers, "Oh my dreams, it's true. They are alive. Oh my, this is so greatly dreamy." Simon smiles and looks at Almont, he says, "Well Almont, I guess the gargoyles are truly home." The wedding march begins for Miss LossDream's walk down the aisle. First comes, the female gargoyles as her bridesmaids and then Miss LossDream in her crisp while wedding gown with a baby pink strip going diagonally across her dress like a sewn in sash of a beauty queen. All the Dreamvillian girls gasp and whispers, "She's so dreamily beautiful, she's going to be a fine queen, I'm so happy for them both, so dreamy." Jilla whispers, "Boys, this is so incredibly dreamy." Almont smiles at Jilla. Simon looks down the aisle as the wedding procession continues. They all reach the wedding alter and take their positions. The wedding goes on as planned. The gargoyles are well accepted as well as the chimeras that carried the groom and brides wedding bands on their heads. The other two were decorated with flowers.

Mrs. Dreamlee whispers, "This is so dreamily amazing. I couldn't have dreamt a better wedding myself." Mr. Dreamlee whispers, "She's wearing one of your designs right?" Mrs. Dreamlee replies, "Why yes she is. I dreamt it up just about a week before she was kidnapped." Mr. Dreamlee says, "Dreamily beautiful."

There's no religion in Dreamville, at least not the organized kinds that exits in the Outsiders world. Dreamvillians believe whole heartedly in their dreams come true that this is enough for their spiritual souls to happily thrive and exists in harmony. They're married by an appointed Dreamvillian dream judge who specializes in marriages. While Miss LossDream and King DreamRoyal stand in front of the Dreamvillian dream judge, the music dies down and the crowds' whispers begin to fade. The Dreamvillian judge waits for complete and utter silence, once he hears absolutely nothing, he turns to Miss LossDream, smiles and he softly says, "Do you Miss Cédrina LossDream take the King and only living heir to the throne as your husband to hold and to keep through sickness and in health, through poorness and richness until death do you part?" Miss LossDream turns to King DreamRoyal and replies, "I Miss LossDream do promise to love and protect you through sickness and in health, through poorness and in richness, through dreams and no dreams should that ever occur again. I promise to love you no matter what for eternity and beyond. I definitely do." Lynelle walks up to Miss LossDream and she picks up the wedding ring from off of her head. Miss LossDream slides the ring on King DreamRoyal's finger and says, "With this ring as our symbol of love, commitment and devotion to each other I be wed to you." All the Dreamvillians are teary eyed with joy. The judge turns to King DreamRoyal and softly says, "Do you King Régimand DreamRoyal the tenth take the Miss Cédrina LossDream, a Dreamtrue School teacher as your wife to have and to hold, to keep protected through sickness and in health, through poorness and richness until death do you part?" King DreamRoyal turns to Miss LossDream, smiles at her and replies, "I King Régimand DreamRoyal the tenth do promise to love and protect you through sickness and in health, through poorness and in richness, I promise to love you no matter what for eternity and beyond. I love you so I definitely do." Miss LossDream smiles cheerful at King DreamRoyal, even though, her eyes are now swelling up with tears, her tears are tears of happiness. Lima walks up to King DreamRoyal and he takes the wedding ring from his head. King DreamRoyal takes Miss LossDream's hand and kisses it before he starts to slide the wedding band on her finger. He lovingly says, "With this ring as our symbol of love, commitment and devotion to each other I be wed to you." The judge softly says, "With the power invested in me I pronounce you as King Régimand DreamRoyal the tenth and Queen Cédrina LossDream DreamRoyal the tenth, King and Queen of Dreamville, man and wife." The judge looks at the king with a smile and says, "You may kiss the bride, your bride." King DreamRoyal smiles at the judge and turns to Queen DreamRoyal. Almont turns to Simon and he whispers, "Brace your-self Simon." Simon asks, "Why?" Jilla says, "They're about to kiss." They all look forward and King DreamRoyal takes queen DreamRoyal by her waist and pulls her forward, towards him, he kisses her on the lips. All of Dreamville cheers as do the gargoyle and the chimeras. Simon somehow is not disgusted by the sight of the passionate embrace. They stop kissing and King DreamRoyal announces, "The wedding supper is in the next outdoor room over. Please everyone come. Oh and come meet our new gargoyle and chimera friends." Simon smiles at the newlyweds as King DreamRoyal winks at him and mouths, "Thank you Simon." Simon nods his head in acknowledgement and gets up with Almont and Jilla to walk to the next outdoor room over. As they walk Jilla daydreams about her dream wedding, she says, "I'm impressed with the royal dream wedding. It was spectacular. I think I want something similar but instead of red, pink, and white roses, I want white lilies. Don't you think Almont?" Almont nervously replies, "Ah yeah, I haven't really thought that far ahead." Jilla says, "Typical, the girl's got to do all the planning. Uh… your hand's getting all sweaty." Jilla releases her grip on Almont's hand and he says, "Oh sorry, I'll get us some napkins." Simon and Jilla sit at a table and Jilla asks, "What's gotten into him?" Simon says, "Oh I don't know maybe all the wedding talk." Jilla says, "Oh maybe. Yeah I'll cool it. I just got caught up in the moment." Simon says, "It's alright, it's just that guys don't think about weddings quite as much or as soon as girls do that's all." Jilla says, "Oh here's Almont coming back. Thanks for the advice Simon, you're the greatest." Almont passes a napkin to Jilla and says, "Here, to wipe your hand, again sorry." Jilla smiles at him and says, "Thank you Almont. Sit down and don't worry, it's all cool." The food gets served and everyone in Dreamville enjoys the feast. Everyone takes there turns meeting the newest citizens of Dreamville. Dreamvillians are impressed with their wit, humor and intelligence. Gargantua takes the hover microphone and says, "Attention, please… Hi everyone in Dreamville…ah…as you all now know I'm Gargantua…" Dreamvillians clap their hands. Gargantua says, "Uh… thanks, thank you…I'd like to say thank you to a very talented dreamer who dreams about the truth, who's known in my small circle as the truth dreamer, Simon Dreamlee. He's another reason to be celebrating tonight too. Not to take away from the royal newlywed couple but I and my fellow gargoyles and our mutual friends the chimeras just want to show our appreciation to you Simon. Thank you." All the gargoyles and chimeras get up on the stage and begin to sing in a rock and roll ballad genre of music. Everyone gets up and slow dances to the song, even Almont and Jilla, leaving Simon by himself listening to the song and lyrics made especially for him.

In the thirteen hundreds we were created.
Then gifted
Immediately misunderstood
By those we were meant to protect.

Lived in exile
Hidden from the world
Captives
Sad

Then came along a truth dreamer
In the twenty-first century
A gifted Simon Dreamlee
Saved us, freed us, we can live again.

Oh Simon Dreamlee we adore you
Oh Simon Dreamlee we love you
Oh Simon Dreamlee we adore you
Oh Simon Dreamlee we love you

Thank you
Thank you
Thaaaaaaaaannk You
Thank you

Then came along a truth dreamer
In the year twenty-ten
A gifted Simon Dreamlee
Saved us, freed us, we can live again.

Oh Simon Dreamlee we adore you
Oh Simon Dreamlee we love you
Oh Simon Dreamlee we adore you
Oh Simon Dreamlee we love you

Thank you
Thank you
Thaaaaaaaaannk You
Thank you

The gargoyles and the chimeras finish their song of appreciation for Simon and all the Dreamvillians cheer. Simon stands up and claps for the Gargoyles. Simon yells, "Awesome, and thank you. Give it up for the gargoyles and the chimeras everyone!" Simon keeps smiling, cheering and clapping. The normal wedding music resumes and everyone either keeps dancing or goes and sits back down at their tables. Simon observes everyone around him and he realizes that he seems to be the only one alone until Almont and Jilla come up to him. Jilla happily says, "So how's about leaving this wedding for a bit of fresh air." Simon says, "Ah nah, I don't want to be the third wheel. At least, I think that's the expression. I'm not sure. Anyway, you two go ahead without me." Jilla says, "Are you sure, we're just going to go play some video games or maybe even jam." Almont says, "Yeah Jilla had this great dream, before everything happened, and it's a duet. Oh yeah I guess that's not three Dreamvillians is it." Simon smiles at his friends and says, "It's alright, go along you two. It's all dreamily cool." Almont says, "See you." Simon says, "Yeah I'll see you." Almont and Jilla hold hands and leave with their parents who are all going to the Alldream's house. Simon's parents walk up to him and he says, "So when are you planning on leaving for home?" Mr. Dreamlee says, "I just want to congratulate the royal couple on their dreamy wedding and then we can go home." His parents go to talk to the royal couple leaving Simon alone again but not for long as Rino and Dee walk up to him holding hands. Rino says, "That's a great song the gargoyles dreamt up for you." Simon says, "Yeah it was. But you know do gargoyles even dream?" Dee says, "I wondered that myself." Rino says, "They have to their living, breathing creatures." Simon says, "Yes but I'd like to find out if they do." Dee says, "Well I don't want to find out right now." Rino looks at Dee and he says to Simon, "Well I guess we're going home. I promised Dee's parents who've already left, that I'd have her home by nine." Simon looks at the hover clock as it goes by and it indicates the time is eight thirty Saturday night. Simon says, "Uh yeah, I didn't realize it was already night." Rino says, "Really, you didn't notice the stars are out and the dance floor's lit by the romantic light of the moon beam?" Simon says, "No, I didn't. My mind must've been elsewhere." Rino says, "Well sweet dreams Simon." Dee says, "Yeah, sweet dreams Simon." Simon says, "Sweet dreams you two. I'll see around some time huh." Rino says, "Yeah maybe, things are ultimately going to change now. So... ah... Bye." Simon says, "Bye." Simon looks around the room and sees his parents are still chatting with the royal couple. He decides to go talk to Gargantua. Simon walks up to Gargantua who's talking with Lionessa. Simon says, "Thanks Gargantua for that great song." Gargantua says, "It's the very least we can do for you." A beautiful, lyrical song begins to play and Lionessa says, "Oh this song sounds nice." Gargantua says, "Would you like to dance with me Lionessa." Lionessa smiles and says, "Certainly." Gargantua takes her hand and they go out onto the dance floor. Simon sees his parents are done their conversation with the royal couple. He walks up to them and he says, "May we please go home now?" Mrs. Dreamlee says, "Yes, son, we're going home now." Simon and his parents walk to their hover car and climb inside. His father starts hovering for their home. Simon looks out the window and Dreamville and all its dreamy dreams that have come true beauty but he feels different. He's not sure how, or what, or why, or when he started feeling this indifference towards Dreamville, Dreamvillians, his friends and even his parents. Normally, he would have jumped at the opportunity to play video games with Almont or had a jam session with Almont and Jilla but this night he just didn't feel like his usual self and his mother notices, she asks, "Simon are you feeling okay." Simon looks at her and says, "Yeah, I feel fine." She says, "You don't seem to be yourself this whole day." Simon says, "You know, I think I'm just exhausted from all the dreamy wedding hoopla and saving the gargoyles, chimeras, King DreamRoyal, Miss LossDream, Jilla, Dee, Almont and myself." Mr. Dreamlee says, "Simon that's no way to talk to your mother." Mrs. Dreamlee says, "It is okay Charles, he's right, he's been through a lot and just had a lot of pressure taken off of his shoulders." Simon says, "No I'm sorry mom, I shouldn't have snapped. I don't know what came over me." Mr. Dreamlee hovers into their hover garage and hover onto the solar panel grid to recharge their hover car and he says, "Thank you son for apologizing to your mother." They climb out of the hover car and go inside the house.

Simon says, "Well sweet dreams mom, dad." His parents holding hands say at the exact same time, "Sweet dreams Simon, our son." Simon walks upstairs and into his bedroom. He pets Boomboom Booya and Frankie Noodles. He takes out his virtualcast from his pocket and places it on his nightstand. He looks out his bedroom window at Wendy, the cow, in the backyard and then sits on his bed for a few moments. He decides to go upstairs to the attic and look around through his telescope.

He walks upstairs to the third floor, the attic and looks out of the window through the telescope. He says to him-self, "Not much for me to see now is there." He looks up into the night sky and sees a view that just a little over a week ago would have freaked him out. The gargoyles are flying through the air while mimicking dancing. He notices that each one has a partner. He says, "How dreamily wonderful for them. Look at that, even the chimeras' dance together." He listens as everyone hovers into their hover car garages and prepare for their sweet dreams. Simon watches as the gargoyles and the chimeras land in the royal couples' yard and nestle into the grass on the ground and go to sleep. Simon looks up into the night sky and wonders. He wonders out loud to himself, "Does she look at the stars at night over there in the Outside world." His cheek's warm, he touches his cheek and he says to himself, "I hardly know her and yet I feel like I've known her forever. My cheek, still feels her kiss on my cheek, her warm, soft lips on my cheek." He looks at the night sky and for fun observes the northern lights which remarkably are visible in Dreamville because of the power of his telescope. Simon quietly says to himself, "I wonder if she can see the northern lights, probably not through all that smog." He hears his mother's footsteps as she comes upstairs. Simon turns around and looks at his mother. She says, "Simon, it's time for bed sweetheart." Simon says, "Okay mom." He gets up and walks to his mother and gives her a hug around her waist. He has no choice because she's a pretty tall woman. He looks up at his mother and says, "I love you mom and dad too." She smiles down at him and says, "We both love you too Simon." They walk downstairs and Simon goes in his bedroom. He closes his door and sits on his bed. He attaches the dream catcher to his head and puts his head on his pillow. He instantly falls to sleep. He instantaneously begins to dream.

Simon's dream fills with music, happy, sad, fun, sad, more sad but overall happy. His dream fills with another stage, this time a stage of the fields where the free gargoyles and chimeras dance, laugh, love alongside of the unicorns and other gentle woodland creatures. His dream fades into the map of the Outsiders world and fades to the MagicDream's mansion. The music notes begin to form on sheet music and lyrics start filling in the blanks of the purpose of the music. The lyrics are hauntingly catchy, truthful, beautiful and memorable, the voice, angelic, sweet, and intoxicating. She sings with heartfelt emotions that can be felt by Simon even while he sleeps soundly and safely in his house, in his room, in his bed. The music swirls in his head and even though he's sleeping, he touches his warm cheek. He feels her warm lips on his cheek. The song's complete and plays in its entirety throughout his sleep until Sunday morning.

We met during your travels in my world.
The world known to you as
Outsiders' world
We met. We touched each other's hearts.

I feel the connection
I know you do too
I feel our friendship blossom into love
Although, forbidden it may be.

We met during your travels in my world.
The world known to you as
Outsiders' world
We met. We held each other's hands.

I feel the connection
I know you do too
I feel our friendship blossom into love
Although, forbidden it may be.

We met during your travels in my world.
The world known to you as
Outsiders' world
We met. We helped each other save our worlds.

I feel the connection
I know you do too
I feel our friendship blossom into love
Although, forbidden it may be.

We met during your travels in my world.
The world known to you as
Outsiders' world
We met. I kissed your warm cheek.

I feel the connection
I know you do too
I feel our friendship blossom into love
Although, forbidden it may be.

Chapter Thirteen – Sunday Morning Of Secrets

Sunday, morning, a full week after the DreamRoyal wedding, Simon wakes and hums the song he's been hearing in his dreams for the past week. He hasn't shared it with anyone, not even Queen DreamRoyal during their musically inclined classes. He's been telling her, Jilla, Almont and the rest of the class that he's still finalizing the previous dream come true about the gargoyles, chimeras and the Dreamvillian kidnapper who happened to be Miss DreamNot once again. In fact, just this past Thursday, he signed a contract with Mr. MakesFilmDreams with a lucrative return once his film's released in the Outsider's world. He knows of one girl that will probably, automatically, recognize the story. He sits up and detaches his dream catcher from his head and looks around his room. Boomboom Booya's on the floor wagging her tail and wanting to be let out of his room. Boomboom Booya barks, "Woof… Woof… Woof" Simon gets out of bed and walks to his door, he opens it and let's Boomboom Booya out. His trusted dog runs downstairs. Simon bends over to pet his cat Frankie Noodles who's purring at his feet. Simon says, "Happy Sunday Frankie Noodles." He hears, "Happy Sunday Simon." He looks up at his mother and says, "Yeah happy Sunday mom." She says, "Well I'm happy to see you're in a better mood. I guess the stress of your last dream come true is finally off your shoulders with that new contract." Simon smiles and says, "Yeah, no more stress." But Simon knows that's not it and his reason for keeping his new song private is because it's all that keeps him close to her. The song's his refuge from Dreamville, his friends and his parents. It's an unbearable yet very endearing reminder that constantly reminds him of her in every way. The warm sensation that was on his cheek is all but faded away but at least his new song will forever keep her memory alive whenever he listens to it. Mrs. Dreamlee says, "What do you have there,

Simon, a new song? May I listen?" Simon replies, "In due time Mom. I'm not quite ready to share this song with anyone just yet. It's … ah…I'm just not willing to share it yet." Mrs. Dreamlee says, "Well I was told that you'd start being secretive as a teenager so okay I'll let this go. You just come find me whenever you're ready to make this dream come true huh." Simon says, "Sure mom, I'll be sure to do that." Simon and his mother go downstairs to the kitchen for breakfast.

Once in the kitchen, Simon sits and eats a raspberry tart with his father. Simon says, "So what's newly dreamed by you?" Simon's dad replies, "Well, I don't know if I should show you son, Why don't you show me yours first?" Mrs. Dreamlee says, "Charles, he's not ready to show his latest dream." Simon says, "Yeah so if you don't want to show me yours then that's cool." Mr. Dreamlee says, "Nah… I'll show you mine. Come on." They as a family go into the virtual viewing room and wake up Viadream when Mr. Dreamlee inserts his computer chip sized hand held computer into the pod slot. Viadream says, "Good Sunday, Happy Sunday Dreamlee family." Mr. Dreamlee says, "Happy Sunday to you too Viadream. Viadream please play my latest dream to come true." Viadream yawns and stretches and says, "With pleasure." Mr. Dreamlee's dream materializes on the hovering virtual screen for their virtual viewing pleasure. His dreams about a new technological gadget that allows Dreamvillians to view the outside world without coming in contact with them at all and without their knowledge of Dreamville and the Dreamvillians. Viadream says, "Dream's over. I'm shutting off unless you want me to play anything else." Mr. Dreamlee says, "No, that'll be all." Simons says, "Sweet….uh…Have a good sleep Viadream." Viadream shuts off. Mr. Dreamlee looks at Simon and asks, "So what do you think son?" Simon says, "I think it's a great invention. I really do! How long do you think it will take to get it patented and in the market?" Mr. Dreamlee replies, "Well this kind of technology gives Dreamvillians a great amount of power over the Outsiders so for now it won't ever be marketed to everyone. It'll probably just be for scientists use so for now keep this top secret Simon." Simon says, "Oh alright. Will you have one set up here at least for our use?" Mr. Dreamlee says, "If I can get it up and running, sure I don't see why not." Simon smiles at his father and says, "That's great dad. That's really great." Mr. Dreamlee says, "Well I guess that's it for this morning. We better get to the summer festivities. Are you coming Simon?" Simon replies, "I think I'll stay at home for this time round." Mr. and Mrs. Dreamlee exit their house and hover to the summer festival grounds. Simon sits in the virtual viewing room and gets up from the couch. He goes upstairs to the attic and looks out of his telescope.

Two hours goes by and for the full two hours he stares out his telescope, every ten minutes or so he increases the intensity of the telescope to view further and further. He reaches the highest intensity possible and says, "Nothing, I can't see the Outsiders world at all. I can't even see up to Miss DreamNot and the ex dream squad chief's black shack in the woods." Simon sits down and for some reason pulls out his virtual communicator that goes off. The image of Almont streams and he says, "Simon, come in Simon." Simon says, "I'm here Almont." Almont says, "Happy Sunday." Simon says, "Happy Sunday." Almont says, "I was thinking I'd bring some games over there to your place and we'd play, you know cheer you up a little. Sounds cool, yes?" Simon says, "Right cool." Almont says, "Alright but I have to drop by Jilla's place first. She wants to see me before she goes and plays for the summer festivities. She's the entertainment for this Sunday." Simon says, "Great for her. How long do you think you'll be?" Almont says, "Half an hour tops." Simon says, "See you in half an hour." Almont says, "Cool. Sign off." Almont's virtual image is gone and Simon puts his virtual communicator in his pocket. Simon walks to his telescope and looks out the window and everything all over again. Simon sees Almont heading in Jilla's house's direction through his telescope. He sees the gargoyles flying towards the summer festivities with the chimeras close behind them. He sits back down and looks at the hover clock as it hovers by indicating the time as ten fifteen on Sunday. Suddenly, his virtual communicator turns on but with no image however with a song, his song that he just dreamt. It's only the refrain but it's still his yet to be revealed refrain.

I feel the connection
I know you do too
I feel our friendship blossom into love
Although, forbidden it may be.

All of a sudden he hears, her voice, the voice he had been longing to hear and was only now beginning to come to grips with the reality that he'd never hear her voice again. Simon takes out his virtual communicator and turns up the intensity of the virtual imaging component and then there she is the virtual image of Diana streams in front of Simon's eyes from the Outside world. Diana says, "Is anyone there, Simon Dreamlee, does this thing work?" Simon turns on his end and says, "I'm here Diana." Diana says, "Wicked cool, I can see a three dimensional miniature version of you." Simon says, "It's really me." Diana says, "I'm sorry if this gets you in trouble Simon but I really needed to talk to you. I kind of miss you." Simon says, "I missed you too. So that's cool." Diana says, "I should tell you that all of the mob woke up and didn't remember a thing, they were all charged with drunken disorderly and the police chief explained that he and his assistant were kidnapped and so Miss DreamNot and the ex dream squad chief were put in a jail. Apparently, they won't be let out for twelve years." Simon says, "That's great news Diana." They both go silent and then Simon asks, "Diana, how did you get a hold of that song and those lyrics." Diana says, "I just thought them up and began singing them. Justin liked the song and my voice and had me record it. That's all I have so far, just those four lines. It sounds more like a refrain really than a song." Simon says, "Ah yeah. It's really good though." Diana says, "I think of you automatically when I play and sing it." Simon says, "Yeah me too." Diana says, "What?" Simon says, "Nothing. Diana, this is great that the Dreamvillian virtual communicator has so much power, we should make time to talk regularly." Diana says, "I think we should do that too." The hover clock hovers by and indicates the time as Ten thirty-five. Simon says, "Diana, you should know that this form of communication between you and me right now is forbidden in Dreamville so keep this and every time we talk between the two of us. Please do this for me." Diana smiles at Simon and says, "I'll do anything for you Simon. I don't want you to get in trouble. I just want to see you and talk to you once in a while. You can count on me to keep it top secret." Simon smiles and says, "I know I can count on you." The hover clock hovers by indicating the time to be ten forty-five. Almont knocks at the door and rings the doorbell. Simon says to Diana, "I have to go Diana but I'll be in touch with you very soon." Diana asks, "When?" Simon says, "Listen and watch for me every Sunday." Diana says, "Okay, every Sunday. Bye." Simon says, "See you and talk to you soon Diana. Sign off." He shuts his virtual communicator. He puts it in his pocket and instead of walking or running downstairs to answer the door he bounces downstairs with absolute joy.

Simon gets to the front door and opens the door. He sees Almont standing with frustration on his face and Simon bounces on him and gives him a hug. Almont says, "What's with the overzealous greeting?" Simon replies, "I'm just incredibly happy today and any day from now on Almont." Almont steps inside Simon's house with a giant smile on his face.

Almont says, "I'm happy to hear that Simon. I was beginning to think you weren't ever going to snap out of your dark place." Simon says, "Oh I think I was never really in a dark place just a distant place but that's about to change drastically for me. Don't worry anymore." Almont says, "Well my best bud we need to get some game playing time done today." They laugh, "Ha-ha. Ha-ha. Ha-ha. Ha-ha." They walk into the virtual viewing room and set up the virtual game player. Simon plays games with his best pal for the rest of the Sunday like a typical Dreamvillian boy despite this being the Sunday of secrets. The best secret, his secret communication with Diana from the Outside world, they're too young to be in love, definitely a close friendship is developing between them but still their contact by any means is forbidden according to Dreamville law. Simon endures not being able to tell his best friend the reason why he's so happy, mostly, because he doesn't want to know what his reaction might be. Almont leaves at four in the afternoon and Simon says, "See you at school tomorrow. Sweet dreams." Almont says, "Sweet dreams." Simon closes the door and the door opens again as his parents walk in from the summer festivities.

Simon's mom says, "Simon, you missed a greatly dreamy summer festival today." His dad says, "Yeah son, it was a good one. Jilla MusiDream's quite talented." Simon says, "Oh I know. Almont and I wanted to play virtual video games. So we did." Mrs. Dreamlee says, "That's great Simon." Mr. Dreamlee says, "Yeah, that's great. Come for supper son." They walk into the kitchen and sit down for some chocolate pie. Simon says, "Great pie!" Mrs. Dreamlee says, "The Dreamchef made this pie. It's yummy." Simon finishes his last morsel of pie and stands up and says, "Well I'll be in the attic if anyone needs me." He turns around and goes upstairs to the attic with the same bounce in his step. Mrs. Dreamlee says, "I think he's going to be okay. He's much happier than he has been during the past week." Mr. Dreamlee says, "I think he's got a boy crush on some girl. That's what I think." Mrs. Dreamlee says, "I thought that too. Wonder who it could be?"

While his parents try and figure out who he's crushing on, in the attic, Simon's taken up a new hobby. Drawing out the map of the Outside world in as much detail as he can remember and based on what he entered in his hand held computer. He draws the rain as well on a separate piece of paper, by the time he's done drawing it, it looks like a piece of art like at the Dreamville Dreams come true Art Museum. Simon sits back and looks at his masterpiece of rain falling and briefly remembers the drops as they touched his cheeks and soaked his clothes yet the rain was so refreshing and revived the greenness of the Outsiders trees foliage. The grass was even greener too. Simon remembered the wind, the force of that wind and the sound of it as it blew by his ears. He remembered the sound of the rain too in combination with the wind. Every miniscule detail is now precious to him and his memory of the Outside world and especially of Diana. He draws another picture. This time it's a picture of Diana. He draws her almond shaped green eyes first and then her cute round nose, her soft rosy cheeks with high cheek bones, her ivory colored skin and her soft, full lips. He draws her brunette hair and all its curls. When he's done, he places all three images into his portfolio and hides it under the table cloth of the table. He stands up and looks outside at the night sky, into the stars and he smiles to himself. Simon says, "Oh dreams, of dreams. I will change the course of history for Dreamville. I've yet to dream how, but when I do I will swiftly act." He changes his focus, stares at the full moon and says, "Most pleasant of nights this dreamy Sunday night. Every Sunday from now will be dreamily cool for me and sweet Diana." Mrs. Dreamlee asks, "Who's Diana, Simon?" Simon's more than startled as he swiftly turns to face his loving mother and he quickly replies, "Mom, I didn't hear you come upstairs." Mrs. Dreamlee replies, "Oh these are my new fashion dream come true, soundless shoes. Aren't they great?" Simon says, "Yeah great. Well I'm going to bed now. Like I should be doing, right?" He rushes past her and downstairs." Mrs. Dreamlee looks around the attic and then follows her son downstairs. Simon's door is already shut and abnormally locked too. Mrs. Dreamlee knocks on Simon's bedroom door. Simon walks to his door and opens it, he says, "Sweet Dreams mom." Mrs. Dreamlee says, "Who's Diana dear." Simon replies, "No one... okay... It's my telescope. I named it Diana." Mrs. Dreamlee says, "Of course dear. Alright, sweet dreams Simon." Simon closes his bedroom door and sits on his bed. He hears scratching at his door. He gets up and opens his door. Boomboom Booya walks inside and jumps on the end of the bed. Simon smiles at Boomboom Booya and just as he's about to close his door, Frankie Noodles zips inside his room. Simon decides to quickly go and get his portfolio of images from the Outside world up in the attic. Once up in the attic he pulls them out from under the table cloth and quickly but quietly runs downstairs to the second floor and into his bedroom. He places his port folio deep in his closet, way in the back behind his clothes. Simon says, "Diana you're my best kept secret. One day we'll be together. One day when we're grown up and adults can't tell us what to do anymore because we'll be adults too." Simon sits on his bed and pets Boomboom Booya. Then he pets Frankie Noodles who purrs. Simon says, "I can't tell anyone, not even Almont. What if I could tell the gargoyles, at least, Gargantua? No I can't risk it. This is my secret and my secret alone that I have to endure just like Diana will be alone in her world out there bearing this very same secret. It's only fair that we both suffer for our loving friendship." Simon's still happy and much more upbeat as he prepares for bed. He hears a knock at his door and says, "Yes, what is it?" Mr. Dreamlee says, "Simon the dream squad cops just returned your hover board." Simon says, "That's great dad. Can you place it in my solar grip hover stand out back?" Mr. Dreamlee says, "Son you can just command it to do that yourself." Simon says, "Oh yeah, right. Cease hover." The board hovers out of Mr. Dreamlee's hands and out the open window of the kitchen and onto the hover stand in the backyard. Mr. Dreamlee says through the still closed door, "Sweet dreams son." Simon replies, "Sweet dreams dad." Simon hears his parent's door open and close. His parents are gone to bed. Simon attaches his dream catcher to his head and promptly falls into dreaming and sleeping once his head touches his pillow. His dream's the same one over and over while he sleeps with a smile on his face. The image of Diana fills his dream. The real one and the one he painted too.

We met during your travels in my world.
The world known to you as
Outsider's world
We met. We touched each other's hearts.

I feel the connection
I know you do too
I feel our friendship blossom into love
Although, forbidden it may be.

We met during your travels in my world.
The world known to you as
Outsider's world
We met. We held each other's hands.

I feel the connection
I know you do too
I feel our friendship blossom into love
Although, forbidden it may be.

We met during your travels in my world.
The world known to you as
Outsider's world
We met. We helped each other save our worlds.

I feel the connection
I know you do too
I feel our friendship blossom into love
Although, forbidden it may be.

We met during your travels in my world.
The world known to you as
Outsider's world
We met. I kissed your warm cheek.

I feel the connection
I know you do too
I feel our friendship blossom into love
Although, forbidden it may be.

How are we to know?
If we're never given a chance to be
Together
Forever forbidden

Meanwhile, in the Outside world, Diana sleeps soundly too in her bed in her inherited mansion with her brother Justin in the next room over and her adoptive family in their individual rooms too. Everything's dreamily dreamy in Dreamville, Simon's home and everything's dreamily dreamy in the MagicDream's mansion in the Outside world, Diana's home. This dreamy Sunday night, they sleep well, soundly and dreamily for now.

Chapter Fourteen – Just Another Monday

Simon wakes up happy, rested and optimistic. He sits up and detaches his dream catcher from his head. He gets out of bed and ticks off the day as one less day to wait before communicating with Diana in the Outside world. He pets Boomboom Booya as she barks at him for his attention, "Woof… Woof… Woof…" Simon says, "Good girl, that's a good girl, Boomboom Booya." Simon walks to his bedroom door and opens the door to let Boomboom Booya out of his room. Frankie Noodles runs past Simon and Boomboom Booya and straight downstairs. Simon follows his dog downstairs into the Kitchen where he greets his parents dreamily and cheerfully. Simon says, "A very happy Monday mom and dad." Mr. Dreamlee says, "Yes Quite, happy Monday Simon. I'm happy to see your positive spirits are back in order." Mrs. Dreamlee says, "Yes me too, happy Monday dear Simon." Simon sits down and eats his blueberry muffin and says with his mouth full, "Dad is there anyway just any Dreamvillian can travel to the Outside world?" Mr. Dreamlee says, "Well son, no there isn't. Traveling to the Outsiders world is strictly forbidden by laws intended to protect us." Mrs. Dreamlee says, "Yes our ancient ancestors had their reasons for establishing these laws and we've always upheld them without question." Simon asks, "Has anyone ever tried questioning these laws?" Mr. Dreamlee looks at his wife and mother of his dear son Simon and he says, "Son, Your mother and I understand that you saw things, many things that don't exist here in Dreamville. The Outside world must be cruel and so un-dreamy." Mrs. Dreamlee says, "What your father's trying to say is that Dreamvillians overlooked the fact that you all came back from being kidnapped and taken into the Outsider's world and this is why no banishment request has been made and you're still free to live here. This is why we wonder why you have thoughts of going back?" Simon knows not to say because his girlfriend lives in that world so instead he says, "I guess my curiosity's getting the best of me. I'll never mention it again." Mr.

Dreamlee says, "Good. That's good Simon. Your life's here in Dreamville with Dreamvillians. Well I better be going and developing my new dream to come true hey Simon." Simon smiles at his father with the knowledge of the looking window in his mind another secret he can't share with his parents and he says, "Yeah dad. Good dreamy luck with that project." Mr. Dreamlee gets up from the table and says, "Thanks son, well I'm gone. See you later." He walks up to his wife and gives her a kiss on the lips. Simon covers his eyes with his hands and whispers, "Nope, still gross." Simon gets up from the table, walks to the back door and says, "I'm gone to school." Mrs. Dreamlee says, "See you later Simon." Simon opens the back door, walks outside into the back yard and closes the backdoor behind him. He walks past Wendy, the cow, and up to his hover board. Simon says, "Hover." He hops onto his hovering hover board and says, "Hover forward." He hovers to the end of their hover driveway and he says, "Hover left. Hover forward." Out of the blue, Gargantua flies up beside him and he says, "Happy Monday Simon." Simon turns and smiles. Simon says, "Happy Monday Gargantua. Where are you going?" Gargantua replies, "Nowhere in particular… Today I thought I'd catch a movie at the Dreamville Theatre." Simon says, "Cool. See you later Gargantua." Gargantua's already flying upward and highly in the Dreamvillian sky but yells back, "See you soon little truth Dreamer." Simon yells, "It's Simon, just call me Simon." Gargantua's high in the sky now but yells back, "Sure thing Simon." Simon looks forward at where he's hovering towards but sees nothing as he strikes another hover boarder and they catapult into the air, Simon soars by Almont. Almont says, "Simon, didn't you see me?" They both hit the ground and watch their hover boards butt into each other in mid air. Simon begins to laugh, "Ha-ha. Ha-ha. Ha-ha. Ha-ha." Almont begins to laugh just because of pure intoxication of Simon's laugh. Finally, Simon replies, "Sorry Almont, I wasn't looking ahead and for hitting you." Almont gets up, walks over to Simon, extends his hand and helps him up. Almont says, "No worries. No one's hurt. We're cool." Simon says, "We're cool." They both say, "Cease hover." Their hover boards hover to them and hover down to the ground. They step on their hover boards and both say, "Hover. Hover forward, Hover fast." Typical, teen aged boys, they race to Dreamtrue School.

They hover into the hover parkade and run into their dreamy school, down the corridor and into Queen DreamRoyal's musically inclined classroom filled with their fellow musically inclined dreamers. Almont runs to a desk besides Jilla and sits next to her. Simon sits in the next desk over on the other side of Almont. Simon says, "Hey Jilla, happy belated dreamy birthday. With everything that happened I forgot about your dreamy birthday being last Monday." Jilla says, "Oh thanks Simon. And... don't worry about it. I didn't celebrate it this year. I was too into the dream royal wedding." Queen DreamRoyal walks into class, looks at the class, waits for everyone to calm down and be silent. Once the students are quiet, Queen DreamRoyal says, "Happy Monday my excellent musically inclined dreamers. Your dreams come true are amazing. Congratulations to Simon Dreamlee for his newest musical production, quite astonishing. Now class, I have some greatly dreamy news of my own to share with all of you. I'm pregnant with the future heir to the Royal DreamRoyal family legacy." All the girls cheer for Queen DreamRoyal as she stands in front of the class and dreamily smiles at their smiling faces while they dreamily smile back at her. Queen DreamRoyal says, "I thank you all so much for being so happy for me. Thank you for sharing this dream with me and making my ultimate lifelong dream come true." Jonas Dreamsound asks, "So you're having a boy?" Queen DreamRoyal replies, "No I'm having a girl." The girls all cheer once again. Queen DreamRoyal says, "Please, please quiet down now class because we now have to get back to business. Who wants to be the next to share their dream come true?" She looks around the room and Jonas Dreamsound puts up his hand. Queen DreamRoyal says, "Okay Jonas we'll listen and view your dream come true. Start when you're ready." Jonas places his hand held computer into the pod on his desk and his dream begins to play.

Hot rhythms,
Dreamvillian moves
Dance to the rhythm of the beat

Hot rhythms,
Dreamvillian grooves
Dance to the rhythm of the heat

Hot rhythms,
Dreamvillian moves and grooves
Dance to the rhythm of the beat and heat

Hot, hot, hot,
Rhythms

Beat, beat, beat,
Rhythms
Heat, heat, heat,
Rhythms

Oh dance to the rhythm, oh hot rhythm
Dreamville
Feel the rhythm in your feet
Feel the heat

Hot, hot, hot,
Rhythms
Beat, beat, beat,
Rhythms
Heat, heat, heat,
Rhythms

Hot, hot, hot,
Rhythms
Beat, beat, beat,
Rhythms
Heat, heat, heat,
Rhythms

Dance to the rhythm of the beat.
Dance to the rhythm of the beat.
Dance to the rhythm of the beat.
Dance to the rhythm of the beat.

Hot, beat, heat, feel, rhythm
Rhythms

At this point, Simon Dreamlee tunes out of the class and thinks about Diana. He thinks about the lyrics of his song and wonders whether or not he should share it but in the end he decides not to share the song about forbidden friendships and love. He comes out of his thoughts as the whole class begins to clap and cheer for Jonas' dream come true. Simon looks around, smiles and begins to clap along with his fellow musically inclined dreamers. Queen DreamRoyal says, "Great dream Jonas. So fun, light hearted, very simple, hot, rhythmically wants to make you dance." She looks around the room and asks, "Who else would like to share their dream today?" The bell rings to indicate the end of the day. Simon looks as everyone flows out of the classroom, on their way to their homes. The day went by like a blur. He doesn't even remember having lunch. Echoing in his head is Jilla's voice, Jilla says, "Simon, Simon Dreamlee, hey Simon." Simon snaps out of his daydream and says, "What Jilla?" Almont says, "Dude, your spacey today like when we talk to you you're totally not paying attention." Simon says, "Ah yeah, you're right. I don't know what's come over me." Jilla says, "I know what's come over you. You miss her." Simon says, "Miss who?" Jilla says, "Don't play dumb with me Simon Dreamlee. You miss her." Simon looks at Almont and then at Jilla and he replies, "Yes, I miss Diana. I think of her constantly. I drew her, I drew all of Newville city and the suburb of Old Newsprings city in the map format and I drew the rain. I don't know why but I feel like I belong in their world more than I belong here in Dreamville." Jilla says, "See now don't you feel better now that you shared instead of keeping it all bottled inside of you?" Simon stands up and looks at Jilla, "Yes, yes actually I do feel much better now that I shared with you two." Almont says, "That's what friends are for Simon." Jilla says, "We're always going to be here for you." They walk out of their class, out of their school and onto their hover boards. Jilla hovers for her home as she says, "Sweet dreams Almont. Sweet dreams Simon." Simon and Almont simultaneously say to Jilla, "Sweet dreams." Simon and Almont race down their street to their crossroads, they both yell, "Sweet dreams." They go their separate ways until they're both home.

Simon hovers into his solar panel grid and says, "Hover down. Cease hover." His hover board hovers downward and ceases to hover. Simon steps off of his hover board. He walks past Wendy, the cow, and says, "Did you have a moo day?" Simon laughs to himself as he pets her. He walks around to the front of the house and enters through the front door. With everything back to normal and the gargoyles and chimeras guarding Dreamville city, no one locks their doors anymore so Simon just walks in with no need of a house key. He doesn't even have to use the finger print recognition security system his father invented when he was only eight years old. Simon wondered about Diana and how she's doing. Simon whispers, "Ah...I talked to her yesterday, I shouldn't be obsessing like this." His mother overhears and asks, "Obsessing about what Simon?" Simon looks up at his mother and replies, "Oh, my new song and sharing it. I don't want to share it because of the memories it evokes in my-self when

I hear and view it." Mrs. Dreamlee says, "Sometimes the most powerful songs can be the most inspiring songs of all. They can be history changing. I think you should share your song as soon as possible." Simon says, "Thanks for your opinion mom. I value your judgement." Simon's mom says, "Well dear son, come have supper." They walk into the kitchen and have a lovely and quiet supper as a family. Simon outbursts into humming as he begins to hear and remember Jonas' song with the lyrics and he says, "Hey Jonas' new composition actually is pretty cool. Rhythmically cool too." Mr. Dreamlee says, "Is that so Simon." Simon looks at his father and replies, "Yeah, I'm only now getting it. I like it." They all laugh. Simon gets up and says, "Well I'm going to the attic until bedtime." He turns around and walks upstairs to the third floor.

Once in the attic he stares out the telescope into Dreamville, observing the other kids parents and the gargoyles. He observes the chimeras and the gentle woodland animals. He observes the unicorns playing with the wild and domesticated horses. Simon whispers, "I do love this place. It's my home. I'm confused. These feelings are confusing me." Simon goes to his bedroom, even though it's only seven, Monday night. He attaches his dream catcher and puts his head on his pillow. He falls to sleep and smiles as he sleeps with his song about Diana flowing through his sleepy thoughts while he dreams. Her image appears and re-appears as the music plays over and over in his mind.

Tuesday morning, Simon wakes up from his restful dreamy dream filled sleep, he sits up and he detaches his dream catcher from his head. Simon gets straight out of bed and walks right to his bedroom door. He walks straight downstairs and out the backdoor to his hover board, he gets on his hover board just as his mother says, "Simon aren't you having breakfast?" Simon looks up at her and replies, "Ah...I'm kind of not hungry this happy Tuesday morning mom but thanks. Hover. Hover forward." Mrs. Dreamlee waves at her Simon as he hovers by, straight forward into the front yard, towards the front street. Simon says, "Hover left. Hover fast." Simon hovers to the crossroads and says, "Slow hover. Still hover." He waits for Almont. Almont hovers towards him and says, "Hover left." Simon says, "Hover right, hover forward." Almont says, "Happy Tuesday Simon." Simon says, "It's going to be once I share my latest dream with everyone." Almont says, "Awesome." They both say, "Hover fast." They hover into the hover parkade, they voice command their hover boards to slow down, and cease hovering. They run into Dreamtrue School and continue to run into their musically inclined classroom. They greet Jilla who's on time as usual. Simon says, "Happy Tuesday." Almont says, "Happy Tuesday Jilla." Jilla looks at both of them and says, "Happy Tuesday Almont, oh, and you too Simon." Queen DreamRoyal enters into the classroom and looks at everyone.

Everyone quiets down and she says, "Happy Tuesday my gifted musically inclined dreamers. I'm so proud to be a part of this group of students' productions and dreams come true. So many contracts and so much praise for your work from the Outsiders, according to our very own, one and only, authorized Dreamvillian who travels from Dreamville to the Outsiders world to market our musical creations. I'm truly, dreamily inspired by each and every one of you as are the Outsiders. In brief, musically inclined dreamers, you're all doing really well according to the Dreamvillian laws implemented by our ancient ancestors centuries ago. Now class, I may seem melodramatic and philosophical this happy Tuesday morning and I probably will be this way for the next while, while I'm pregnant so bear with me and we'll all get through this dreamily. Okay… who wants to share their latest dream to come true?" Simon looks around at everyone in the class but no one's raising their hand to volunteer their latest dream. Simon notices Almont looking at him as well as Jilla. Simon hesitates to be the first to showcase his dream due to its content and suggestion of Dreamvillians lack of freedom to be with whoever they want to be. Just as Simon's about to raise his hand, Brunei Dreamilee raises his hand. Queen DreamRoyal says, "Brunei Dreamilee, please go ahead, make your dream come true." Brunei nods his head, places his computer sized hand held computer in the pod on his desk and his dream materializes on the screen and is heard by all in the class. His dream's pure classical music with simple piano playing in the background as an angelic male voice sings the lyrics.

Rivers calming
Oceans waves
Sea sunsets rosy pink
Nothing's better than here
Being here with you

It's so lovely here with you
It's so enchanting my being with you
It's so meant to be, us, you and me
It's so lovely here with you

I wouldn't want to be anywhere
But here
Right here with you
Beaches soft sand through my toes
Your toes too

It's so lovely here with you
It's so enchanting my being with you
It's so meant to be, us, you and me
It's so lovely here with you
I'm so happy here with you
But I don't think it matters
Where I'd be as long as
I'm with you
Being with you

It's so lovely here with you
It's so enchanting my being with you
It's so meant to be, us, you and me
It's so lovely here with you

It's so lovely here with you
It's so enchanting my being with you
It's so meant to be, us, you and me
It's so lovely here with you

It's so lovely here with you.

The class claps and cheers for Brunei and queen DreamRoyal claps and she says, "Lovely, Brunei. Great piano piece, I love the pure, simple piano music as the only musical instrument in this piece. I can hear this sung like you just dreamt it but also like an opera in an opera style production. What do you think Brunei?" Brunei replies, "I think that everyone clapped for it so it's likeable." Queen DreamRoyal says, "Oh it's more than likeable, it's loveable and very marketable." Brunei says, "Thanks Queen DreamRoyal." Queen DreamRoyal looks around at the rest of the class and smiles at each and every one of the students while she waits for the next volunteer. A few minutes go by and she says, "Well class, who would like to go next?"

Almont and Jilla both look at Simon and Simon caves in to their inquisitive looks. Simon raises his hand and says, "I'll go next Cédrina, uh, I mean Queen DreamRoyal. Pardon me." Queen DreamRoyal laughs and says, "Ha-ha. Oh Simon Dreamlee, that's quite alright. I was hoping that you'd have something to share with us soon. I wasn't expecting it to be so soon but go ahead, when you're ready." Simon says, "Okay, give me one moment to set up." He takes out his computer chip sized hand held computer and places it in the pod on his desk. He looks up at the class and then at Queen DreamRoyal and as confidently as he can he says, "Now, you're all aware of my past controversial dreams come true that eventually after much debate came true so I'd like you all to keep that in mind as you view and listen to my next and latest dream to come true. Please enjoy as I'm truly putting my heart out on display as if I were wearing it on my sleeve." Queen DreamRoyal says, "Sounds interesting Simon. It also sounds like you're not ready to let us hear and view your dream." Simon says, "I'm not but my dreamy mother said to me last night that dreams can change the course of history, I've experienced one of those types of dreams and now I'd like to share another." Simon looks at everyone quietly waiting for him to start his dream to come true. Simon says, "Play my latest dream." His dream plays in full with the final verse that he dreamt only that past Monday night.

We met during your travels in my world.
The world known to you as
Outsiders' world
We met. We touched each other's hearts.

I feel the connection
I know you do too
I feel our friendship blossom into love
Although, forbidden it may be.

We met during your travels in my world.
The world known to you as
Outsiders' world
We met. We held each other's hands.

I feel the connection
I know you do too

I feel our friendship blossom into love
Although, forbidden it may be.

We met during your travels in my world.
The world known to you as
Outsiders' world
We met. We helped each other save our worlds.

I feel the connection
I know you do too
I feel our friendship blossom into love
Although, forbidden it may be.

We met during your travels in my world.
The world known to you as
Outsiders' world
We met. I kissed your warm cheek.

I feel the connection
I know you do too
I feel our friendship blossom into love
Although, forbidden it may be.

How are we to know?
If we're never given a chance to be
Together
Forever forbidden

Or will new attitudes allow
Freedom
Outsider and Dreamvillian
To love
To grow
To be together
Forever true

Simon's dream ends and the room lights up again. His fellow classmates clap and cheer for his dream but Simon knows the suggestions in his dream are, without a doubt, going to stir up a brand new controversy in Dreamville city, with his fellow Dreamvillians of all ages, even if King Régimand DreamRoyal the tenth and queen Cédrina LossDream DreamRoyal are progressive in their thinking, to dare think of a relationship between an Outsider and a Dreamvillian is absolutely frowned upon and forbidden to all Dreamvillians according to the ancient doctrine that no one dares to alter, not even to adapt to the changing times and attitudes. Jilla and Almont hold hands as they get up from their desks and stand by their friend Simon's side while his newest, latest dream replays and is streamed by his fellow Musically inclined dreamers for all Dreamvillians to hear.

The End

Epilogue

Simon celebrates his fourteenth birthday with Almont, Jilla, Rino, King Régimand DreamRoyal the tenth and Queen LossDream, Booya, Frankie Noodles, his parents and his brand new friends the Gargoyles and Chimeras. He spends the year preparing his ultimate dream to come true, all the while he still dreams and releases other more light hearted and dreamy pieces of music throughout the year.

Simon's hard at work and secretly keeping in contact with Diana MagicDream as he had promised he would do and she does the same. He wishes he could confide in someone, anyone but he doesn't risk taking that chance and again withholds information about himself from his best friend Almont.

Despite this, Almont and Simon's friendship grows and becomes stronger with each passing dreamy Dreamvillian day. Almont and Jilla's romance blossoms rather nicely too. Simon's interest now don't lie with the telescope but with the girl from the Outsider's world, the forbidden world that he longs to now get to know better, freely and safely without the threat of banishment from his beloved Dreamville, his parents and his friends. Each virtual communiqué he takes is another chance of being caught and cast out forever.

Simon spends the year in dreamily wholesome Dreamville being tormented by the pull he feels for the Outsider girl and her beloved world, this despite her lineage to Dreamville. Instead of worrying he focuses all is energy into his next production based on his dream to come true.

Author Bio

R. E. Brémaud earned her bachelor of arts degree from the University of Manitoba with a major in English literature and three minors in French literature, history, and psychology. She resides in Manitoba, Canada. This is her second book.